"Oh, give me a break," I said. "You want me to believe that you and Gregor and those guys are a bunch of blood-sucking bats?"

"Got something to show you," Justin said. He came close to me and opened his mouth. "See my teeth? Nothing special about them, right? Now watch."

His canines began to grow. They just came out of his upper jaw and hung there in his mouth, like stalactites. Then, slowly, they went back in again.

"Don't be scared," he said.

ALSO AVAILABLE FROM DELL LAUREL-LEAF BOOKS

VAMPIRE HIGH

DOUGLAS REES

Published by
Dell Laurel-Leaf
an imprint of
Random House Children's Books
a division of Random House, Inc.
New York

Visit us on the Web! www.randomhouse.com/teens

Educators and librarians, for a variety of teaching tools,
visit us at www.randomhouse.com/teachers

ISBN: 0-440-23834-X

RL: 4.8

Reprinted by arrangement with Delacorte Press

Printed in the United States of America

First Dell Laurel-Leaf Edition August 2005

10 9 8 7 6 5 4 3 2 1

OPM

To Jo, who knew the ending before I did,
and
to Karen Wojtyla, a fine editor

VAMPIRE HIGH

STUCK IN NEW SODOM

This all began on the day I came home with straight Fs. F in English, F in math, F in social studies, F in science. I'd even managed to get Fs in gym and homeroom. I was proud of that.

My parents, however, weren't.

"What is this?" my father raged when I showed him my grades.

"A report card," I said. "They put these letters down on it, see, and it tells you what grade you got."

"I *see* the letters," he said. "And the comments with them. 'Cody has turned in no homework at all for nine weeks.' 'Cody has been absent or tardy every day this quarter.' Oh, this one's a classic. 'Cody has spent every day in class trying to prove that Sir Isaac Newton was

1

mistaken about the law of gravity. These experiments have consisted of repeatedly jumping off my desk and flapping his arms. This is distracting to the other students. He has done no other work.' And homeroom. There is no comment from your homeroom teacher, so I suppose I'll have to ask you—how on God's green earth did you manage to flunk homeroom?"

"Easy. I never went," I said.

"And what's this?" said Dad. "A special note from the principal? Yes. 'Your son has shown the intellectual development of an illiterate hurdy-gurdy grinder and the attention span of his monkey. It is impossible to evaluate his work as he has not done any. He is lazy, sly, and generally useless. I confidently predict he will be spending the rest of his life in ninth grade. I only hope it will be at some other school. Go back to California.'"

That last part sounded like good advice to me. But I doubted Dad would take it.

We glared at each other in that way we'd developed ever since he'd moved us from home to this dump of a town, New Sodom, Massachusetts. He wouldn't drop his eyes and I wouldn't drop mine.

This was Mom's cue to stop making terrified little gasps and whimpers and start making excuses for me. I liked this part.

"It's not his fault, Jack," she said.

Right.

"It's this place."

Right again.

"He's been miserable ever since we moved here."

Three rights. Dad's out.

But Dad didn't know he was out.

"Beth, he's cutting off his nose to spite his face," he said. "I can't accept that."

Yeah. And you can't do anything about it, either.

Dad threw back his head like he was about to explain to a jury why only an idiot wouldn't see things his way and give his client what he wanted.

"Now, look here, young man," he said. "This move is the best thing that's ever happened to us. I was going nowhere at Billings, Billings and Billings. Jack Elliot was good enough to handle their really tough cases, but not good enough to promote. No, my name wasn't Billings, so that was that. When this opportunity opened up at Leach, Swindol and Twist, I knew it was the best chance I'd ever get to have the career I wanted. So here we are. And here we stay. And you'd better get used to it."

Fine. And I will go right on flunking. And you can get used to that.

I didn't say it. I only thought it. But I meant it.

Dad looked at my report card again.

"Homeroom," he said softly. "My son flunked home-room."

Mom came over and put her arms around me.

"It won't do any good to get mad, Jack," she said. "These grades are a cry for help. Cody needs something in his life to connect to. He needs something to love."

Good idea, Mom. I would love to go home.

"Extracurricular activities, perhaps," Dad said. "Working on a road gang after school. Freelance garbage collection. He needs to acquire a skill with which he can support himself, since college will obviously be out of the question."

3

"That's not fair," Mom said. "You dragged us three thousand miles from home to further your career and you expect us both to accept it as though nothing has happened. Well, that's not realistic."

Now it was "us." This was sounding pretty good. Better than usual. Maybe enough "us" would get me back to California. I thought about doing the stare again but dropped my head instead.

"And another thing," Dad said. "That hat is an obscenity."

He must have thought Mom had made a good point. He was changing the subject.

"That hat goes," he said. "At least don't wear it in the house."

This was my Black Death baseball cap, which I always wore backward because Dad hates baseball caps worn backward.

"Don't change the subject," Mom said. "You're not in court now. Cody needs something in his life to care about."

"All right, all right," Dad sighed. "Tell us, Cody, can you think of anything you want that would make you happier?"

"Tattoos."

Dad crumpled up my report card.

"I partially agree with you, Beth," he said. "Our son does need something new in his life. He needs a tougher school. Tomorrow I'll start making inquiries."

The next day I was so worried that Cotton Mather High started to look almost good to me. The cracked ceilings, the wooden floors that creaked like they were in

4

pain; even the boys' bathroom, which was as dark as a grave and smelled worse. The thought that I might never see them again made them seem almost friendly. No, that wasn't true. It was just fear that, bad as this was, Dad was determined to find someplace even worse.

When he came home that night, he had a thin smile on his face and a couple of big manila envelopes in his hand.

"Seek and ye shall find," he said. "I have learned that there are not one, but two really hard schools in this excellent town. I've got all the information right here."

"You work fast," Mom said, crossing her arms.

"It turns out that there are other members of my law firm who have children in each one," Dad told us. "Clancy Kincaid has a son and daughter in Our Lady of Perpetual Homework. He speaks very well of it. And there's a public school that's just as good and even harder to get into—Vlad Dracul Magnet School. Hamilton Antonescu's daughter goes there."

Our Lady of Perpetual Homework?

My stomach froze. I'd heard about that place. Every kid in town was afraid to be sent there.

"But—but we're not even Catholic," I squeaked.

"That isn't necessary," Dad said with satisfaction. "Many of their most difficult students come from other religious traditions. Sooner or later, everyone breaks. Or so Clancy Kincaid assures me."

I believed it. I'd been by the place once, when I was cutting class. They said you could hear the screams coming through the walls. I hadn't, but I'd never forgotten the words carved in the stone over the door:

ALL HOPE ABANDON, YE WHO ENTER HERE
—DANTE

"But—it's expensive, isn't it?" I said. "I mean, private school—"

"Easily affordable," Dad purred. "I'm making a great deal more money than I ever did at Billings, Billings and Billings. But I gather you would rather go to Vlad Dracul, if you can qualify."

I didn't know. I'd heard of Vlad Dracul, but only the name. The kids at Cotton Mather never said much except things like "The football team's up against Vlad this Saturday. Pray for them."

When I'd heard that, I'd asked the kid who'd said it what the big deal was.

"Shut up," he'd explained.

"Come on, what is it? Is Vlad Dracul where they send the kids who flunk out of Our Lady of Perpetual Homework?" I'd asked.

"Look, stupid," the kid had said. "Never say those words. Never say the whole name. And no, it's not where they send kids who can't cut it at OLPH. No real parent would ever send their kid to Vlad."

And that was as much as anybody had ever told me.

"What kind of name is Vlad Dracul for a school?" Mom said.

"What do you mean?" Dad asked.

"I mean," Mom said, "that Vlad Dracul was a vicious, cruel fifteenth-century Romanian monarch who impaled his prisoners alive on stakes. What was the school board thinking of?"

"There appears to be a sizable contingent of Romanian Americans in this town," Dad said. "Antonescu tells me that among the Romanians, Vlad the Impaler is quite a hero. Obviously they named a school after him as a gesture to ethnic pride."

"Well, among the rest of us he's better known as Dracula," Mom said.

"So what?" Dad said. "The school has the highest GPA in the state. Not only that, but the kids who graduate from it go on to top universities. Not just some of them. All of them. Every year."

"I don't want Cody going to that school," Mom said.

"Then it's Our Lady of Perpetual Homework," Dad said. "Either one is fine with me."

"Do I get anything to say about this?" I asked.

"I don't see why you should," Dad said. "Given that we're having this conversation because of your demonstrated unwillingness to meet the most minimal academic standards. But, that said, sure, go ahead. What do you want to say?"

What do I want to say? Don't do this to me? Take me home? Yeah, but that isn't going to happen. Not tonight, anyway.

"How about hiring a private tutor?" I said. "Maybe about twenty-five and good-looking."

"Thank you for your suggestion," Dad said. "We're going to visit a couple of schools tomorrow."

VLAD DRACUL MAGNET SCHOOL

From the outside, Vlad Dracul Magnet School looked almost normal, just nicer than most public schools. Okay, it looked nicer than any public school I'd ever seen. But remember, this was the outside I'm talking about. Only the outside.

In the first place, the campus was huge. The buildings were just scattered around, with lots of space between them. And there were lots of trees. All the buildings were of shiny yellow brick, and a road ran all around them. There were two one-story buildings for the elementary school with a big thing that I guessed was the cafetorium between them. And there was lots of expensive-looking playground equipment covered with snow.

A narrow road with trees on both sides separated the

playground from the middle school, which was two two-story buildings. Then there was another road and the high school. This had five big buildings with words like CLASSICS, SCIENCE, and THEATER carved over the doors. Then a little farther on there were three more buildings, looking like mansions, set facing each other.

"Is this really a public school?" I asked Dad.

"The finest in the state," Dad said. "Or so Antonescu tells me. Looking at this place, I can well believe it."

He parked the car in the high school lot and we headed for the first building. A sign near it said THE OFFICES MAY BE FOUND WITHIN, TO THE IMMEDIATE LEFT OF THE DOORS.

Those doors. They glowed like gold as we went up the steps. They looked like they must weigh a ton apiece, but when we touched them, they swung open without a sound.

And what I saw then made the outside look like a slum. There were black marble pillars and red marble pillars and white marble floors and walls. There were crystal chandeliers and big oil paintings that showed a lot of guys waving swords at each other. The classroom doors were made of some kind of expensive-looking wood that smelled good.

We went through the first door on our left. Inside was a silver-haired woman behind a desk that looked big enough to land a plane on. The carpet had a design in it and looked like it might take off for a quick flight, and the walls were paneled in more of the expensive-smelling wood. There was even a fireplace.

"I beg your pardon," Dad began. "My name is Jack—"

"Please do come in, Mr. Elliot," the secretary said. She stood up, and I thought she must be about seven feet tall. "Principal Horvath is looking forward to meeting you and your son." She had one of those real smooth New England accents. Her *r*s were almost *h*s.

She turned to me.

"And you would be Master Cody? Welcome. I am Ms. Prentiss, Mr. Horvath's secretary."

She held out her hand to me and I took it. I was surprised. Her handshake was strong, real strong.

Then she touched a button on her desk. "The Elliots are here, Mr. Horvath."

The door behind her swung open—another door that opened without a sound—and Mr. Horvath came out.

He was even taller than Ms. Prentiss, and he shook both our hands like we were friends he hadn't seen in years.

"Mr. Elliot and son. Please come in. Be seated. We must talk," he said. And he put his hand on my shoulder and guided us into his office.

There was an even huger desk, an even bigger fireplace, a sofa, a couple of easy chairs, and a window closed off by heavy drapes.

There was also something on the floor that I guessed had to be a dog because it raised a head the size of a Volkswagen, opened a mouth full of steak knives, and made a noise that was somewhere between a chuckle and a growl.

I jumped.

"This is Charon," Mr. Horvath said. "He likes you. Come, Charon."

The thing got up on its plate-sized feet and came over to me. He sniffed me all over like he was searching for drugs. Then he stared at my face with huge yellow eyes.

"Karen?" I said. "Good dog, girl. Nice doggy."

"No, no." Mr. Horvath smiled. "His name is *Charon*. The Greek deity who rows the dead across the River Styx to the underworld."

"What—what breed is he?" I managed to whisper. "German shepherd, maybe?"

"Timber wolf," Mr. Horvath said.

Charon looked at Mr. Horvath, wagged his tail just once, and went back and lay down.

"He's out of a particular Canadian strain," Mr. Horvath went on. "They tend to be larger than the average for the breed. Some place in British Columbia. What's its name? Ah, yes, Headless Valley. But enough about that."

He waved his arm at the sofa. "Sit down, please, Mr. Elliot and son. We are here to discuss educational matters, not subspecies of wolf."

We sat. Mr. Horvath took one of the chairs and made a sort of tent with his fingers. "So. You are seeking admission to our school, Master Cody," he said.

"Uh—yeah," I said.

"Do you swim?" His eyebrows went up.

"Some. I got my Red Cross beginner's card before we moved," I said.

"Excellent. The Red Cross. We are very supportive of that organization. Blood drives," he said, like they were the best idea anybody ever had.

"Now," he went on, "as you know, we are a school with very high standards. Extracurricular activities are

11

as important as academics. Every student must participate. Would you be interested in joining our water polo team?"

I didn't do sports, so I didn't say anything. Water polo, for pete's sake?

Dad spoke up.

"Cody would certainly be willing to try out," he said.

"I should like to hear Master Cody's views," Mr. Horvath said.

"Well, I don't know," I said. "I'm not real into sports. I don't think I'd be very good."

"That is of no importance," said Mr. Horvath. "Willingness is everything. Victory and defeat—what was it Whitman said? 'Battles are lost in the same spirit in which they are won.' It is the spirit that is precious to us here."

As if. The only thing any principal ever cared about was winning. Every kid figures that out in the first ten minutes in junior high.

"Suppose I try out and don't make it?" I asked.

"As I said, the willingness is everything," Mr. Horvath said.

"So if I try out, I get into the school?" I asked.

Horvath nodded.

Okay, I had it figured out. I try out for the team, which gets me into the school and gets Dad off my back, and saves me from Perpetual Homework. Then I flunk the water polo tryouts, which won't be hard since I don't even know how to play, and go out for something easy. Like the Game Boy team. Dad's happy, Horvath is happy, and I'm no worse off than I was.

So I said, "Okay."

"Excellent," Mr. Horvath purred. "I am happy to inform you that you are accepted to this school."

Dad frowned. "Perhaps you'd like to see his grades?" He held out my last two report cards.

"Not necessary," Mr. Horvath said.

"I'm afraid his grades aren't very good," Dad said, sort of waving the cards at him.

"It is not how we begin but how we end that matters," Mr. Horvath said. "Many students come to us with low grades. None leave with them."

He reached over and shook my hand again. "Welcome to Vlad Dracul, Master Cody," he said. "Practice is at two-thirty. Report to the natatorium during free period today to receive your equipment."

"The what?" I sort of mumbled.

"Ah. Excuse me. The swimming pool. Calling it the natatorium is one of our traditions. We are a very traditional school in some respects, very progressive in others."

Dad was still frowning. "Frankly, Mr. Horvath, when Hamilton Antonescu told me about this school, he gave me the impression that the admission standards were quite strict."

"They are extremely rigid," Mr. Horvath said.

"But you haven't even looked at my son's records."

"I'm afraid I don't regard report cards from Cotton Mather High as an indication of a student's potential, Mr. Elliot." Mr. Horvath smiled. "Your son's record in California was quite good."

"You have his California records?" Dad said. "How?"

"By requesting the transcripts," Mr. Horvath said.

"But we only came in the door five minutes ago," Dad said. "I didn't tell anyone I was going to apply here. We only decided last night."

"You did inquire of Mr. Antonescu about us, did you not?" Mr. Horvath said. "He informed us of your possible interest. We made the request in the hope you would apply."

"Overnight?"

"We live in a wonderful age, do we not, Mr. Elliot?" Mr. Horvath said.

"But—"

"Mr. Elliot, Mr. Antonescu recommended you to us, as a colleague of his. His own child is already here. He himself is a graduate. That recommendation, your son's record—his *total* record—and his willingness to participate in water polo are sufficient qualifications to enter our school. I congratulate you."

Mr. Horvath stood up. So did Dad. So did I. Mr. Horvath shook Dad's hand again, opened the door to his office, and said, "Ms. Prentiss, have we Master Cody's schedule of classes?"

"Right here, Mr. Horvath," she said.

There was a little white card on her desk, printed in gold. The whole thing was printed, even my name.

ELLIOT, CODY
FIRST PERIOD HOMEROOM 7:45–8:00 KOVACS
SECOND PERIOD MATHEMATICS 8:05–9:00 MACH
THIRD PERIOD ENGLISH 9:05–10:00 SHADWELL
FOURTH PERIOD SOCIAL STUDIES 10:05–11:00 GIBBON

FIFTH PERIOD GYMNASIUM 11:05–12:00 LUCAKCS
SIXTH PERIOD DINNER 12:05–1:00
SEVENTH PERIOD SCIENCE 1:05–2:00 VUKOVITCH
FREE PERIOD 2:05–2:30
WATER POLO 2:35–3:30 UNDERSKINKER

"What exactly is free period?" I asked.

"It's time at the end of the day to visit your teachers and ask for help with anything you perhaps didn't understand in the lesson," Ms. Prentiss said. "Or to visit the library. Or even to visit your friends in the student union."

"The student union?" I said.

"It's that large square building between the dormitories," Mr. Horvath said.

"What kind of public school has dormitories, Mr. Horvath?" Dad asked.

"One with a worldwide reputation, Mr. Elliot," Mr. Horvath said. "One that attracts students from many countries."

"And the taxpayers support this?"

"I am happy to say that the citizens of this community have voted us whatever we have asked for, for generations," Mr. Horvath said. "Usually by margins approaching ninety-nine percent."

Dad looked at me and I knew what he was thinking. I was thinking it, too.

What kind of school is this?

"Now, Mr. Elliot, if you are satisfied, please sign your son's schedule of classes," Mr. Horvath said.

Dad took out his pen, but he didn't sign.

"We still haven't visited OLPH," he said.

"Dad, sign," I said.

Water polo had to be better than perpetual homework. Besides, I wouldn't be on the team that long.

Dad signed. As he left, he mumbled, "Call me."

I knew from his tone that he meant "Call me if anything too weird happens," and I felt warm toward him in a way I hadn't for months.

HOW TO MAKE THE
WATER POLO TEAM WITHOUT
EVEN TRYING

When Dad was gone, Mr. Horvath turned to me.

"Master Cody, I want you to know how pleased I am that you have decided to enroll here. Please feel free to visit me any time you are confused or uncertain about the practices of our school. I am sure you will find some of them odd at first, and I want you to be comfortable here."

"Thanks," I said.

Then he called, "Charon," and the giant timber wolf slinked over.

"As this is your first day, I will assign Charon to show you to your classes," he said. "Don't worry. He knows his way around this school better than I do."

Then he said something to Charon in another language. The wolf walked over to the office door and looked back over his shoulder at me.

I followed him down the hall, trying to keep as far away as I could. That wasn't very far, though. Every time I got more than a few feet behind him, Charon would stop and wait till I caught up.

So in a couple of minutes I was at the door of my math class. I turned the handle—the doors had gold-colored handles, not knobs—and went in with Charon right behind me.

In a way, Mr. Mach's math class looked like a regular classroom. In another way, it looked like no classroom I'd ever seen. There were blackboards, windows, chairs, and desks, just like any classroom you've ever been in. But the blackboards were real slate—stone so dark the chalk marks on it almost glistened. The chairs were armchairs; the desks were real desks, with drawers and glass on top and individual lights. The students needed them. The glass in the windows was tinted so dark that it was almost like trying to look through a fourth wall.

Of course, everyone turned around when I came in. There were only twelve kids in the whole class, and they almost all looked alike. They were tall and pale with straight black hair and dark eyes. Hardly anybody seemed average sized like me.

I did notice one kid, brown-haired with glasses, who seemed real short. His name was Justin Warrener. I knew that because he had a name plate on his desk. Every kid did.

"Come in, Elliot," Mr. Mach said. "You'll find your desk over there by the window. Put your things in the cloakroom and join us. We were just discussing some of the remarkable mathematical properties of the Aeolian scale."

By now, I was almost not surprised that he already knew my name.

Mr. Mach was a tall, heavy guy with bushy black hair and a beard that looked like it wanted to wander off on its own. He had great eyes, really friendly-looking. He was holding a violin in his hand.

While I took off my hat and coat and put them away in the cloakroom—which was a real room, with individual coat hangers and places to sit—and yeah, my name was already on one of the closet doors—I heard him draw the bow across the strings and make a long, pure note.

"That's B, of course," Mr. Mach said. "But just think about this: If I place my finger so, and make the same stroke with the bow, it becomes A. What's changed? It's still the same instrument, the same man playing it. What's different?"

"The rate of vibration?" I heard a girl's voice ask.

"Exactly," Mr. Mach said. "The vibration rate, which is the rate of the quavers in the string itself. We can number these, divide them into halves and quarters—they're infinitely divisible, in fact—and compute the mathematical profile of any given note."

I took my seat as quietly as I could. Charon sat beside me with his ears cocked forward like he was really paying attention. I noticed that his head was on a level with mine.

"Let me restate my main point for Elliot's benefit," Mr. Mach said. "I am demonstrating to the class why it is that music was—properly—regarded as a branch of mathematics by our ancestors. Music is math you can hear."

"Gotcha," I said.

A couple of kids giggled, and Charon gave me a disgusted look.

While Mr. Mach talked, I quietly checked out my desk. When I pulled open the top drawer, I found a math book, a notebook, pens, pencils, protractor, ruler, calculator—everything laid out and waiting. There were even extra batteries for the calculator. If I had wanted to learn anything, this would have been the place to do it.

I didn't, but with Charon sitting next to me, I thought I'd better look like I was interested. I pulled out the notebook and a pen and wrote, *Music is math you can hear.* Then I sat trying to look as though I knew what Mr. Mach and the rest of the class were talking about.

At the end, Mr. Mach said, "Your homework for Friday is to select any composition by Mozart. Assign numeric values to the parts of the composition and, using fractions, not decimals, demonstrate how they interrelate mathematically."

Friday? This was Wednesday. These kids were going to turn in homework like that in two days? The only thing I knew about Mozart was that they made a movie about him. I'd seen it with my parents. He wrote some music and he died.

Then I heard a deep, soft gonging sound roll through the hallway. The other kids got up and filed out quietly.

I hung back and waited till the last of them were gone.

"Mr. Mach," I said. "Just so you know, there's no way I can do that assignment. Where I was in school before, we were doing algebra."

He smiled and looked at me with those great eyes.

"You can try. When you've tried, you'll know more than you do now. Don't worry about it." He clapped me on the shoulder. "Nice to have you in my class."

So I went out. I reminded myself that I really wanted to flunk anyway, as long as I could do it without getting sent to good old Perpetual. It looked like I wasn't going to have any trouble.

The hall was full of kids, but it was weirdly quiet. Hardly anyone talked. If they did, it was in whispers. Nobody shoved, nobody ran. They just headed for their next classes down that beautiful hallway, through those silent doors.

Charon took me to a room across the hall. I checked my schedule. English. Shadwell.

As I went in, a broad man with a huge bald head bounced across the room to me and grabbed my hand.

"Elliot! Glad to meet you, boy. Have a seat over there by Antonescu. Check your desk. I think you'll find everything in order, though. Any relation to T. S. Eliot, by the way? No, I suppose not. I see you spell it differently. Still, a great poet, eh? Despair, despair, but beauty, too. 'I should have been a pair of ragged claws/Scuttling across the floors of silent seas.' Great stuff. And Pound. My God, Pound. Have you read the *Cantos* yet?"

He sort of pushed me down into my seat.

"Now, just briefly, let me explain what's expected of you this year. We're all writing something. A play, a novel, a volume of poems, perhaps an epic. I'm very fond of epics myself. Written seventeen of them so far. Dedicate them to my wife. She loves that. Always bakes me a lasagna whenever I finish one. Must have you over some night to feast. But enough about that. The main point is, you can write whatever you choose, but it must be finished work, and of a suitable length. Say, three hundred pages on average for the novel or epic, full-length plays, that sort of thing. Tell you what, though, since you're coming in at the middle of the year, I'll let you get away with rewriting some of your early work. What is it that you write, exactly?"

"Nothing," I mumbled.

"Nonfiction?" Mr. Shadwell bellowed. "Why not? History, biography, that sort of thing. Rather you didn't try to fob me off with a scientific treatise, though. Not my strong suit. Still, if you offer me something on plate tectonics, or radio astronomy, or Triassic paleontology, I should be able to pick my way through it."

"No, I said, 'Nothing,'" I said.

"Ah," said Shadwell. "Water polo, I take it?"

I nodded and held out my schedule.

"Never mind. Forget I said anything," Shadwell said, handing it back.

There was another deep gonging sound.

"Time for class," Mr. Shadwell said. "Good talking with you, Elliot."

He turned away and I heard him mutter, "Water polo. Why didn't they say so?" Then he sort of pranced to the head of the class and over to a podium with a huge bound pile of paper on it. The pile was as thick as three phone books.

"There are certain principles of Anglo-Saxon prosody that I consider to be absolutely critical for those of you engaged in writing poetry," Mr. Shadwell said. "And they are of value to any writer. I find them to be well embodied in my latest completed work, *Quetzal,* which, as you know, traces the course of Mexican history from the erection of Teotihuacán around 150 A.D. to the revolution of 1910. Therefore, I will proceed to read a portion of it to you, illustrating the points I wish to make as I go."

He opened the thing to the middle and started to read.

I didn't know what it was about. I caught something about a battle, and that sounded interesting, but I couldn't figure out who was doing what to who, and then the fighting stopped and everybody started suffering. I gave up even trying to listen, though it was hard not to because he bellowed.

Charon didn't seem as interested as he'd been in Mr. Mach's class, either. He turned his back on Mr. Shadwell and curled up with his tail wrapped over his nose. I was pretty sure he was sleeping.

I looked in my desk. It was a lot like the one in Mr. Mach's class. There was a big book, *Some Glories of English Literature, Collected by Norman Percival Shadwell,* and a notebook and pens. The difference was that every drawer of this desk was filled with paper, and there were five drawers.

And these kids were all writing *what*? I'd never written anything longer than a birthday card without being forced.

I looked around the room. The other kids all looked like they were listening. Geez, they were serious. I saw the little brown-haired guy from math class taking notes like mad. Then I looked at the desk beside me.

"Sit next to Antonescu," Mr. Shadwell had said. Well, Antonescu's first name was Ileana, and she was beautiful. She had pale skin and long black hair, like most of the people at Vlad Dracul, but she was short and delicate. Her eyes were almost as yellow as Charon's. When she moved, it was like a bird flying, even if it was just folding her fingers around her pen.

Was she Hamilton Antonescu's daughter? This could be good. If our dads worked together, and her dad had already helped get me in here, maybe she'd want to be my girlfriend. I could use one.

So I passed her a note.

Hi. I'm Cody Elliot. I'll bet you're Hamilton Antonescu's daughter, right? My dad works with your dad.

I slid it over to the corner of her desk when Mr. Shadwell dipped his head down to get a start on an extra-good bellow, but she didn't notice. It just sat there while she looked at him with her chin resting on her folded hands.

Every time he stopped reading to holler something about how important this passage was to Anglo-Saxon prosody, and how well what he'd written showed it, she'd pick up her pen and write a few words, then put it down and turn her beautiful eyes back to him.

Then class was over. Ileana stood up and started to walk away. For the first time, she noticed the note. She read it, gave me a funny look, and walked off with it tucked in her purse.

That was the first time I realized that so far, no kid had talked to me. And no kid did, not in social studies, where Mr. Gibbon, who looked like one—a gibbon, I mean—talked for fifty-five solid minutes about the salt

trade in early Carolingian Europe, and for homework assigned us to bring salted food to class. Not in gym, which
at least seemed like a normal class with jumping jacks
and running and a coach who kept screaming at us.

Then it was time for dinner—not lunch—and Charon
and I went with all the other kids toward the student
union.

When I walked in, I saw . . . a palace. I'd never been
in a palace before, but I knew I was in one now. Cin-
derella, Sleeping Beauty, and Snow White must all have
ended up in some place like this.

Tapestries and carved wood covered the walls. The
ceilings were painted with scenes that looked as though
they probably came out of one of Mr. Shadwell's epics,
and there were huge pieces of gilded furniture, suits of
armor, and statues everywhere.

And that was only the lobby.

Everyone went to the left, into a dining hall—no, a
banquet hall—and sat. There were tables for four with
place cards and red tablecloths and black plates and cups
and shining silver.

Charon led me to a place with my name on it. Then
he went back toward the kitchen. I saw one of the waiters—there were waiters in white jackets—call the chef
out of the kitchen. The chef bent over and Charon licked
him. The chef laughed, and in another minute Charon
was eating a pile of meat the size of a steer off a silver
platter.

As soon as we were all sitting down, the waiters
wheeled out carts loaded with covered dishes. They
glided over to the tables, put the food in front of us,

whipped the covers off the plates, and gave us little bows.

"Bon appétit," the one at my table whispered.

The food was stuff I'd never seen, eaten, or heard about. Little slices of meat, bits of cheese. Vegetables that looked like they'd been imported from Mars. But, I had to admit, everything tasted great. Maybe they had a secret sauce.

I was sitting with Ileana, Justin Warrener, and a big kid named Brian Blatt. He had real short hair and lots of acne.

"You the new guy?" he said to me.

At last, somebody talking to me.

"Yeah," I said.

"You on the water polo team?"

"I guess," I said. "I told Horvath I'd try out."

"Hell," said Brian Blatt, and put his face down near his plate and started to suck his food up his nose—okay, I'm exaggerating that part. But that was all he said.

As soon as he'd finished licking his plate and stealing all the rolls from the basket in the center of the table—all right, he didn't lick his plate, but he did steal the rolls—he got up and shuffled out the door.

Some other guys sitting together at a table in the corner got up at the same time.

"Hey, dudes, wait up," Brian hollered.

They hollered back, " 'S'up, dude?" and "Whuzzit?"

At last, normal conversation. But they went out together and the dining hall was quiet again. The loudest sound was the silverware clinking over the soft hum of the other kids' talk.

Ileana put down her fork.

"I beg your pardon," she said.

"Huh?" I replied.

"You placed a piece of paper on my desk today," she said. "Will you kindly explain why you did that?"

She had some kind of accent, just barely there. Her words were very precise.

"It was just . . . a note," I said.

"I see. And is this behavior common among students at other schools?" she asked.

"Everybody does it," I said.

"I see. Thank you," Ileana said, and started eating her dessert. It was some kind of food nearly like ice cream, but better.

"So are you Hamilton Antonescu's daughter?" I asked.

"Yes," she replied.

"I'm Cody Elliot," I said. "My dad works with your dad."

"So you said in your note," she said.

And that was that.

After a few minutes, the other kid, Justin, spoke up.

"I've been told other schools are noisy places. Everyone talking all the time. Is that true?" he asked.

"Yeah," I said.

"Then why do you pass notes?" he asked.

" 'Cause you don't want anyone else to know what you're saying," I said. "Notes are private."

Justin shook his head. "Doesn't make much sense. Do the teachers make you pass the notes?"

"No," I said. "We're not supposed to do it."

"Makes even less sense," he said.

"Doesn't anybody ever pass notes here?" I asked.

"What for?" Justin asked.

"Well, like I said, so you can tell somebody something you don't want anybody else to know," I said.

"Such as?" Justin asked.

"Well, anything," I said. I wasn't going to tell him you pass notes to girls to get them to pass notes to you. If he couldn't figure that out, it wasn't my job to explain it to him.

After lunch—I mean dinner—ended, we all got up and went to class. Ileana and Justin melted into the rest of the kids, and Charon came back. We were surrounded by people who didn't seem to notice us.

At first, I wondered if they even noticed each other. Then, as I watched them longer, I saw that they did. They were talking in clusters, or even walking hand in hand. But they were so quiet, so turned toward each other, that they were like water flowing around me.

All of them, except for a few mousy brown-haired ones like Justin, seemed to be tall, pale, and dark-haired. And they almost all wore sunglasses. Whipped them on as soon as they got outside.

"So what do you think?" I asked the wolf. "Am I going to like it here?"

Charon stopped. He gave me the kind of look he had given me in the principal's office. Then, slowly, his tail made a small circle.

What was that about? Yes? No? Anything?

I decided to ask another question and see what happened.

"Hey, Charon," I said. "Is this school as hard as it looks?"

He stopped again and looked back over his shoulder. His tail moved side to side, high up.

Could be yes, could be no, could be nothing.

"Is it hot today?" I asked.

His tail swung back and forth low, brushing the snow. He gave me a disgusted look.

If that means anything, it means no.

"Charon, do you like me?"

The tail didn't move. Then he kind of snorted, jerked his head toward the school, and started walking.

I followed.

If Charon was talking to me, I figured I knew four words: *yes, no, maybe,* and *none of your business.* But how smart was he, really? Smart, obviously, but that smart?

Science class was Ms. Vukovitch, a blue-eyed blond giant who looked like all the women in the ancient movies my parents love to watch. She came into the room like a supermodel on parade, looked me over once, flashed us all an electric smile, and talked about the stars for forty-five minutes like she was dishing the dirt on them.

Then she told us, "You know, guys, that the star Betelgeuse is four hundred, six hundred light-years away. Nobody knows for sure. You probably think that's far enough. But it's a red giant, and it's gonna go supernova one of these eons. Can't help it, it's just what stars like that do. Blow up, collapse, end of story. But let's face it, when that happens, we could get toasted. Anyway, for tomorrow, I want you to calculate how long it will take before Betelgeuse does that, how long after that before the first effects are felt on Earth, and how extensive those effects will be. And don't forget to include the Van Allen Belts in your computations. See you tomorrow."

I flipped through the pages of the science book I'd been given. The chapters on astronomy might as well have been written in Swedish.

I shook my head.

"Man," I said to Charon. "I couldn't pass here if I wanted to."

Then came free period. I went to the student union, where I stood against the wall with Charon and watched a roomful of people ignore me. When it was finally time, the wolf led me to the gym.

The natatorium took up one wing of the gigantic gym and had its own entrance. When I went in, I noticed there was no connection between it and the rest of the gym complex. It just looked from the outside like it was all one building.

There was an Olympic-sized pool and bleachers way up near the ceiling, on top of the locker rooms. Six guys were standing around near the diving boards in black trunks with red slashes on the front. They were Brian Blatt and the others he'd walked out with at dinner. They just looked at me from across the water.

Charon led me to the locker room. There was a sort of office in one corner of it. It had a beaten-up desk, a swivel chair, and a huge lump of suet sitting in it that I guessed must be Coach Underskinker. He was asleep, with a case of beer beside him. It was empty.

Charon growled. The coach opened one eye.

"Whaddya want?"

Charon growled again.

"Oh. Yeah. They told me you was comin', punk. Okay, wolf, I'll take it from here."

He swung his feet down, discovered the floor with them, and pushed himself up. "C'mon, punk," he said. "I gotta give yuh yer equipment."

I followed him into the depths of the locker room. There were hundreds of lockers there, but it looked like most of them had never been used. Only a few at the end had padlocks. The rest hung open, empty.

Underskinker stared at the lockers as if he was trying to remember why we were there. Then he picked one.

"Yer six-ninety-six," he said. "Remember it."

"Six-ninety-six," I said.

"Well, open it," Underskinker said. "I ain't gonna do everything for yuh. Geez."

Inside 696 was a black bag with a red slash on it and everything I needed. Trunks, soap, towels.

"Getcher trunks on an' go inna pool," Underskinker said. He started back up to his office.

"Don't I have to try out or anything?" I called after him.

"Don't bodduh me," he answered without looking back. "I'm busy in duh office."

I got dressed and went out to the pool.

The guys I'd seen when I came in were still standing around. Charon was gone.

For a couple of minutes, we just stood looking at each other. Then I went over to them.

"Hey," I said.

No answer.

" 'S'up?" I tried.

Nothing.

"I'm Cody Elliot," I said.

"So?" This was from Brian Blatt.

So we all just stood there for a while.

Finally a scrawny red-haired guy who was obviously part weasel asked me, "What'd Underskinker say?"

"About what?" I asked.

"What'd he say after he gave you your locker?" the semiweasel shouted.

"He said, 'Don't bother me, I'm busy in the office.'"

The guys started high-fiving each other and shouting.

"No school today!"

"We're still skatin', man!"

"Dry as a bone!"

"Yeeow!"

They started down to the locker room, slapping each other on the back. I followed them.

They all started putting on their clothes, shouting about how they didn't have to swim.

"So that's it?" I asked Brian.

"So that's what?" he asked.

"That's practice?" I said.

He put his forepaw on my shoulder. "Look. Punk. You want to get in the water, get in the water. You want to go home, go home. You want to go to hell, go to hell. Nobody cares. I don't care. We don't care. Underskinker don't care. You got it?"

No. I didn't get it. But I got that Brian wasn't going to explain it any better than that.

I went back out and looked at the pool. It was green and huge and all mine if I wanted it.

Hell with it. I like swimming.

I went over to the low board and dived. I swam to the end of the pool and back again. It felt great to be warm, to be floating, to be in control of something, of me, my own body, in water. It was like California. I felt so good I wanted to cry.

Instead, though, I swam back and forth until I'd swum out the tears and a lot of the fear I'd been feeling all day. Maybe this place wouldn't be so bad if I could end every day like this.

By the time I walked out of the natatorium, I was almost happy.

HOW TO BECOME
A MARKED GADJE WITHOUT
EVEN TRYING

Charon was gone, all right. I saw a couple of his big paw prints in the slush a little way away from the gym. He was done with me.

It was the end of the day now, and kids were everywhere. Some were going in and out of the student union; some were getting picked up.

I saw a line of black stretch limos with VLAD DRACUL MAGNET SCHOOL written on the side and kids lining up to get in.

I saw plenty of other cars, beautiful cars, cars like I'd never seen before, all driven by chauffeurs. And just one or two kids getting into each of them.

Wow. Dad's never going to be satisfied with his Mercedes again.

The scream came from behind me.

It was a boy's scream, but high and wailing. Whoever was making it was really scared.

I looked back. I saw a big, dark wall of kids looking at something and I went toward them.

The scream came again.

When I got to where the other kids were, I saw Justin Warrener. He was about four feet off the ground, twisting in the grip of four huge, pale, dark-haired guys who each had hold of an arm or leg. His glasses were gone, his face was red, and I guess they'd taken his coat.

But what were they going to do with him?

There was a small creek trickling a little way behind the student union. I mean, small. I doubt if it was a foot deep at this time of year. It looked like these guys had broken the ice on it and were going to dump Justin in.

It didn't look dangerous—how could it be? But Justin was screaming like he'd just missed the last lifeboat on the *Titanic*.

And every kid watching was doing just that—watching. Nothing else. They were like a wall, a wall with sunglasses.

Have you ever done something without thinking about it—I mean something you've never done before and maybe would never do again—and had it change everything that happened after that?

That's what I did then. Without thinking about it, I bent over and made a quick snowball and threw it at the tallest guy.

"Hey!" I said. "Put him down."

The big guy turned around.

"Who did that?" he asked. He didn't even sound angry.

"Let me give you a hint," I shouted, and put the next snowball right in his face.

He let go of Justin's leg and gave it to his buddy. Then he came over to me.

"Do you know who I am?" he asked.

"Yeah," I said. "You're the jerk who needs help to beat up Justin Warrener."

In the crowd behind me I heard a soft laugh. Just one.

The guy was head and shoulders taller than I was. He looked like he was made of muscle, and he already had a beard.

I was beginning to feel nervous.

"Put him down," the guy said.

The other three guys dropped Justin into the snow. He got up and scampered off.

Then the big guy, the one who looked like he was considering whether or not to eat me, grabbed me with one hand and lifted me off the ground.

"You do not know me, gudgy," he said. "And for that reason, I may be merciful. Permit me; I am Gregor Dimitru." He cocked his head and held me out at arm's length. "No, actually, I do not think I will be merciful."

And he threw me, I mean, actually threw me, to the next guy, who caught me one-handed and pulled my face next to his.

"Vladimir Bratianu," he shouted, and tossed me to the third guy.

"Constantin Trifa," he shouted, and tossed me to the fourth.

"Ilie Nitzu." This guy grinned and threw me back to Gregor.

"And what is your name, gudgy?" he asked, holding me over his head now.

"Put me down," I managed to say.

This was hell and nightmares come to life. These guys were handling me like I was nothing. I *was* nothing to them. I could feel it.

"Putmedown?" Gregor said. "I don't think I ever met anyone named Putmedown before. Where are you from, Putmedown?"

"I think he means he wants you to put him down," the one named Vladimir said.

"Ah. Perhaps so, Vladimir," Gregor said, like he was thinking it over. "What do you say, Putmedown? Is he right?"

He shook me.

"Yes," I said with my teeth rattling.

The next second I was flying through the air. I landed hard at Ilie's feet. He used one of them to kick me. I bounced like a soccer ball.

I couldn't believe this was happening. Why had I ever thrown those snowballs? Why wasn't anybody helping me? Where was that damn wolf? Could I even escape?

I got to my feet. Someone shoved me from behind, right into Gregor, who held me off the ground again and slapped me on both cheeks while I squirmed and twisted.

Then my left foot connected with his crotch and he suddenly went even whiter than he already was.

"Agh," he said, and dropped me.

I was still scared, but I'd hurt the guy. Something fierce carried me forward, and I pitched into him with everything I had.

This worked for about one second, until one of the others pulled me off.

"Kill—kill him," Gregor gasped.

I think they might have, too, but suddenly there was someone standing beside me. Someone shorter than I was. I felt a firm hand on my arm, and then a sharp fingernail marking an *X* on my cheek.

"I mark this gudgy," Ileana Antonescu said in a quiet voice.

All four guys stopped moving like someone had pulled their plugs. They looked at Ileana like they didn't believe what she had just done. But they also looked like there was nothing they could do about it.

Gregor straightened up.

"As you will, princess," he said. And he gave her a little bow.

Gregor turned away and went back toward the student union. Vladimir and Constantin put their hands on his shoulders, and Ilie fell in beside them.

The wall of watching kids began to break up with hardly a sound.

Ileana took her hand off my arm.

"You will be all right now," she said. "You will be safe."

Then she was gone, too.

I didn't know what to say to her. I didn't even know what to think. The whole thing felt like it had happened in a movie, a bad movie.

What had made those guys so strong? What had Ileana meant when she'd said she marked me? And what was a gudgy? In fact, what the *hell* was a gudgy?

My shoulder hurt where I had landed on it, and my spine hurt where Ilie had kicked it. At least I hadn't screamed for help. And I'd hurt Gregor. For one second I'd been winning.

But as I looked at the messed-up snow and the backs moving away from me, I felt completely lost, homeless, and alone.

"Oh, God. God," I said to myself.

"Thank you," a voice behind me said.

It was Justin. He had his jacket and glasses back. He had a sort of smile on his face, as if he was trying it out to see if he liked doing it.

"That was the nicest thing anybody's ever done for me," he said. "I hope you're all right."

No, I am not all right. I am about as far from all right as I have ever been.

"I'll live, I think," I said.

"Oh, you'll live all right," Justin assured me. "Now Ileana's marked you, you're safe, even from them."

"What do you mean, marked me?" I said. "What the hell is going on at this school?"

Justin gave me a funny look. "You mean you really don't know, gudgy?"

"Don't call me gudgy," I said. "I don't even know what it means, but I know I don't like it."

Justin shook his head. "*Gadje,* not gudgy," he said. "It just means—it means you're not one of us."

"One of who?"

He took a deep breath. "It means you're not what some folks call a vampire."

"Is that supposed to be a joke?" I said. "Because it's about as funny as a busted crutch."

"It's not a joke," Justin said. "It's just what we are."

"Oh, give me a break," I said. "You want me to believe that you and Gregor and those guys are a bunch of blood-sucking bats?"

Justin flinched. "It's a lot more complicated than that."

"But you want me to believe it."

"Got something to show you," Justin said. He came close to me and opened his mouth. "See my teeth? Nothing special about them, right? Now watch."

His canines began to grow. They just came out of his upper jaw and hung there in his mouth, like stalactites. Then, slowly, they went back in again.

"Don't be scared," he said. "I'd never hurt you. Besides, you're marked. By tomorrow the whole school will know."

"I have to go," I said.

Vampires! Vampires were real, and one was talking to me. Telling me not to worry because another vampire had marked me. The only reason I didn't run away right then was that I couldn't move. Justin went on and on, telling me there was nothing to worry about, I was safe, I was set, but I didn't want to hear it. I didn't want to stand there in the snow in the fading dirty light anymore. I wanted to be someplace safe and warm and far away.

Finally, when I thought I could do it, I tried moving my legs. They worked.

"I'll walk with you to your coach," Justin said.

I'd have as soon strolled with a sidewinder, but I wasn't going to say so. I'd do anything he said just to get out of there alive. So I walked along beside him with my hand sort of up by my throat. I couldn't help it.

As we crossed the campus, Justin said, "You can ask me some questions if you want. I figure I owe you."

"Is everyone here a—vampire?" I said. "All of you?"

"We don't call ourselves that," Justin said. "We think it's kind of an insult. We call ourselves jenti. Always have. It means 'people.' We're mostly v—jenti here. But there's always a few gadje, anyway. We need 'em to keep the water sports going."

"But why do you just want us for water sports?" I said. "That doesn't make any sense."

Justin looked down. "It's complicated. Basically, jenti don't like to be in water much. You could say we hate it. But water sports are part of the state curriculum."

"So the other guys on the team are all gadje?" I asked.

Justin nodded.

"And Coach Underskinker?"

"Him too."

"But they don't even get in the water," I said. "And Underskinker is a drunk."

"Doesn't matter as far as the state's concerned," Justin said. "All you guys have to do is lose a few games during the season, and the rest of your lives are taken care of."

"Taken care of how?" I asked.

Justin snorted. "I mean you don't have to do homework ever again. You don't even have to try. You're going to pass with straight As. When you graduate, you'll go to a good college, one we control. You'll graduate from that, playing water polo on scholarship, maybe. Then we'll see you get a good job. In Hollywood, or with some big law firm. And there's always politics."

I could feel the hard, frozen ground falling away under my feet. None of this was real. It couldn't be. Vampires were for movies or Halloween. But everything Justin said made sense of this weird day, even if none of it made sense at all.

"How long has this been going on?" I asked, trying to get my mind around the idea.

"Oh, New Sodom's been here over three hundred and fifty years," Justin said.

"You mean the Pilgrims were vampires? I mean, jenti?" I said.

"I don't know about the Pilgrims," Justin said. "My family were Puritans. And we've been here right along. Everybody knows which families are which, and we all get along pretty well. Now."

"But not always?"

Justin sighed.

"There were some bad times. The gadje tried to burn us out in the 1640s. And the 1650s. And the 1660s. And there was kind of a war between us in 1676. The whole town was ruined. Then everybody took a look at how few of us were left on both sides and decided no one was going to win. So we all swore to the New Sodom Compact. The gadje would stop trying to wipe us out, the jenti wouldn't—you know, *drink*—any closer than Boston. So things were pretty peaceful. We all went to the same schools and things. Just didn't have anything to do with each other that we didn't have to. Then in the nineteenth century the new jenti started coming in, the Transylvanians and the rest. The gadje started to get scared again. So we worked out a new deal. We separated more. We got our own school, for instance. And we pretty much shop in separate stores and things like that. It works."

The hairs on the back of my neck were standing at attention.

"So—does everyone else know? I mean in the rest of the state?"

"It's no secret," Justin said. "But nobody talks about it, either. It works better that way. Anything else you want to ask?"

"A-about how many?" I asked. "Here."

"Maybe fifteen thousand," Justin said.

Fifteen thousand vampires in my new hometown. And I was in their own special school. No wonder the kids at Cotton Mather hadn't talked about this place.

I had to get out of here. Even Dad wouldn't keep me in a school full of vampires. No, that wasn't quite true. He wouldn't keep me in a school that he believed was full of vampires. But how could I make him believe it? There was no way, short of inviting Justin home and asking him to do his thing with his fangs.

Then I had another thought. Straight As for no work. A guaranteed future. And Justin had said I was "marked" like it was a good thing. And there was that New Sodom Compact. Maybe I was really safe. And maybe I could make this into a really good deal. I began to feel just a little less frightened.

"That thing Ileana did, marking me," I said. "What was that about?"

"You'd better ask her," Justin said, blushing.

"Come on," I said. "You said you owe me."

"I can't tell you that," Justin said. "It's just an old custom. Ileana's family's kind of old-fashioned."

There was only one limo left now. The back door swung open as we approached.

"How do I know this is mine?" I asked.

"Just tell the chauffeur where you want to go," Justin said.

I got in.

"Thanks again," Justin said. "Maybe you'd like to come over sometime."

"Oh. Yeah," I said. I wasn't going to say anything that might disappoint him.

"Where to, Master Cody?" asked the chauffeur, who looked about nine hundred years old and probably was.

"To 1727 Penobscot Street," I said.

The car purred away from the curb.

I looked back through the rear window at Justin. He was still standing there, watching me. That wispy little smile came back to his face and he raised his hand.

For some reason, so did I.

VAMPIRE CANDY DREAMS

When I got home, Mom was cooking dinner. I could smell she was making corned beef without the cabbage. Corned beef is one of my favorite foods.

"How did it go today, boy of mine?" she said. She sounded so happy, I knew she was worried.

"It's real different," I said.

"Good different, or bad different?" Mom asked.

"Very different," I said. "Is there time for me to have a bath before dinner?"

"Lots of time," she said.

I went upstairs to the bathroom. I ran the tub as hot as I could stand it, poured in Epsom salts, and eased into the scalding water.

Our tub was huge. I could sink up to my chin with nothing sticking out.

I really, really, really needed to think. And right now I didn't think I could. My mind was running back and forth like a rabbit caught between two coyotes. I remembered what Justin had said about vampires hating water, and that brought back that horrible moment when Gregor and his buds had thrown me back and forth like the rag in a game of steal the bacon, and I started to shake.

I couldn't stop. My muscles just took over and did what they did. My teeth chattered. I lay in the water and watched it slosh out of the tub. Maybe I made some noises. I don't know.

It was funny, though. Once the shaking stopped, I felt better. It was like my body had thrown off its fear to get me ready for the next thing, whatever it was.

I got out of the tub and mopped the floor with a towel. Then I examined my back in the mirror. My shoulder was already deep purple, and so was the place where Ilie had kicked me. But the scratch Ileana had put on my cheek was almost gone.

I took a couple of aspirins, went across the hall to my room, and put on some sweat pants and my UCLA Bruins shirt. Then I flopped on my bed.

I heard Dad come home. He and Mom started talking. Part of it sounded like it was about me. I had to tell them something about today, but what?

I went downstairs.

"Hello, son," Dad said. "How did it go today?"

"Pretty weird," I said.

Then the phone rang.

Mom handed it to me, smiling. "It's for you, Cody," she said. "It's a girl."

I took it into the family room to have some privacy.

"Hello?" I said.

"Hello, Cody Elliot?" said a high, precise, beautiful voice.

"Yeah, hi, Ileana," I said.

"When you threw the snowballs this afternoon and helped Justin to escape from those boys, he came and found me and asked me to help you. I did the first thing I could think of, and I want to explain it," she said. "It is an old custom among my people—my ethnic group—and I want to make sure that you understand it. It means nothing to me—that is, it does not mean to me what you may hear it means from others. So I need to clarify."

"Great," I said.

"Justin called me and told me you had asked."

"Yes?" I said.

"In the old times, a jenti and a gadje might form a sort of partnership," she said. "Its sign was a mark on the gadje's cheek. It meant that the gadje was under the protection of that particular jenti, and all other jenti would respect that. It is not done much anymore, but we still honor it when it is done. So you do not have to worry about Gregor and those others any longer. That is all I wanted to say. That and to thank you for trying to help Justin today. He is my oldest friend."

"Wait a minute," I said. "You mean you put your mark on me to protect me, but you didn't mean it?"

"No, no," she said. "I am explaining this badly. I meant that part. It is the rest you should disregard."

"What rest?"

"As I said, it is a very old-fashioned custom."

"What's the rest?" I said again.

"I prefer not to say," she said, sighing.

"Justin said I should ask you. So I'm asking. Tell me," I said.

"It is nothing. Just that in the old days, very far back, there was the protection for the gadje, and there was also what the jenti got." She was talking fast.

"What was that?"

There was a long pause. Finally she said, "Blood."

It was like I'd already known it. The last piece of the puzzle. I wasn't even scared.

But Ileana went on. "That is the part that must not concern you. I do not want you ever to think of it again. Please do not."

"Okay," I said. As if anyone could not think about being another person's private blood bank. "But there's one more thing I really need to know."

"What is it?"

"Are you and Justin going together?" I asked.

"Oh, no," said Ileana. "We are just friends from our first days, that is all."

"Then . . . maybe you'd like to go out with me sometime?"

There was a pause that went on for about a week.

"A relationship?" she said finally. "Thank you very much, but no. I do not think so. I do not think we are the same kind of person. But I like you. I think you are a good gadje. You were very brave this afternoon. Thank you for saving my friend."

Click.

"You're welcome," I said to no one.

I put the phone down and went back into the dining room.

As soon as I came back, Mom brought dinner in. We all sat down and she lit candles.

It was the candles that made me decide not to tell much about what had happened at school. Candles meant she was happy. It had been too long since I'd seen her like this.

Dad noticed it, too. He brought out a bottle of his best wine and opened it. He and Mom raised their glasses.

"To you, Cody," Dad said. "At the end of a long day." He reached across and poured some into my empty glass.

I'd had wine a few times before but never Dad's good stuff. I tried it and tasted oak, dust, and the sun of a summer day years ago.

"Not bad," I said.

"A hundred and twenty dollars a bottle and he says 'not bad,'" Dad said. "We're raising a connoisseur."

"Who was that on the phone?" Mom asked.

"Ileana Antonescu," I said. "Something about school."

"You have some classes with her?" Dad asked.

"A couple."

Dad leaned forward. "How is that place, anyway? What happened after I left?"

"Well, it's pretty much like a regular school," I said. "The work's harder and the teachers are weirder than at Cotton Mather."

"Sounds promising," Dad said.

"Did anyone show you around, at least?" Mom asked.

"Yeah."

"How do you think you're going to like it?" Dad asked.

"I can't say," I said. I drank the wine, feeling it coat my tongue. When my glass was empty, I held it out.

"Just a little more," Dad said.

But that little was enough. My head started buzzing. I could hardly keep my eyes open. And even though I was hungry, I just didn't feel like eating.

"Excuse me," I said, getting up. "I'm going to bed."

"I'll leave you a snack in case you wake up later," Mom said.

I did wake up later. I don't know how much later it was. My room was pitch-black, the house was quiet, and clouds had covered the whole sky.

I just lay there, feeling my bruises and listening to the wind make the trees sigh a little.

Time seemed to have stopped. It felt like morning would never come and it didn't matter that it wouldn't. I was safe now.

Now I could think.

I couldn't decide whether I had just fallen into the best deal of my life or the worst.

I wouldn't have to worry about grades, or working, for the rest of my life. Ileana had protected me from every other vampire at Vlad Dracul. All I had to do was mark time until the vampires got me into college—a California college, I'd see to that—and then I'd never have to leave home again.

So what was making me sick about it?

I tossed, I turned. No matter how hard I tried, I couldn't figure out what was wrong. I went over it again and again in my mind. Getting As without trying. College without trying. Even a job without trying. What was the catch?

After a long time, I began to wonder if I shouldn't stay home the next day, since I wasn't getting any sleep. It made a lot of sense to me.

"Why not?" I finally said to myself. "It doesn't matter whether I go or not."

And then I drifted off, just in time to hear my alarm start buzzing.

I can't do this today.

I staggered downstairs to the phone. The brochure for dear old Vlad Dracul was right next to it, and the phone number was on the front cover.

"Vlad Dracul High School," said Ms. Prentiss's soft voice.

"This is Cody Elliot," I said. "I'm calling in sick today."

"Oh, dear," said Ms. Prentiss. "Well, just get better, Master Cody."

As easy as that, I was home for the day.

"Cody, are you not well?" Mom asked, looking worried.

"Just tired. I didn't sleep," I said.

"Frankly, Cody, I was beginning to hope you'd found a school where you'd get down to work," Dad said.

"Get off my back," I told him. "I have all my assignments. And if I don't pull straight As in the next nine weeks you can send me to military school."

I slammed the door to my room and threw myself on the bed. Sleep took me back.

• • •

I woke up early that afternoon and stretched. I still hurt, but the places I didn't hurt felt good.

I'd had a stupid dream about Horvath. I'd been sitting in his office, and he'd been right up in my face, smiling and feeding me candies. They were soft little candies, very sweet, and he kept popping them into my mouth, one after the other. The thing was, I didn't like the taste. I'd woken up because after I'd swallowed the first couple, I'd just been holding them in my mouth and my mouth had gotten full.

I laughed. I bet Horvath would have done that for me, as long as he needed me in his school.

I decided I was hungry and got up.

The house was empty. There was a note on the table. Mom had gone to the store.

I wandered through the rooms, feeling good. Today I could do whatever I wanted.

I had to find out when the water polo games were. Other than that, my time was my own. Maybe I could work from home. Not that I had to do any work.

I wondered what colleges in California had enough vampires on their boards or whatever that I could just waltz into them. And scholarships. I'd have to apply for some of them, just to make everything look right.

I looked out the back windows. The sky was still gray, the ground was still white, and the trees were still black. I could feel the scene sort of wrapping around me, getting inside. I looked into those clouds and it was like I could see my future for years ahead. Just clouds and more clouds, but I'd be flying through them, floating. I wouldn't have to do a thing.

By now, Justin and Ileana would be in seventh period, probably going over their homework on Betelgeuse. I'd have bet they'd been up till midnight doing those assignments. But, hey, they were vampires. They probably preferred midnight.

Anyway, tomorrow I'd go back to school and I'd hand Ms. Vukovitch a blank sheet of paper. Maybe I'd write the word *Betelgeuse* on it so that she'd know which assignment it was supposed to be. I'd get it back with an A. I'd hand Mr. Mach a sheet of paper that said *I don't know anything about Mozart* and get an A. Shadwell—I'd give Shadwell a piece of paper at the end of the year that said *This is an epic* right in the middle of it and get my A. Social studies: A. Gym: A. Water polo—who cared? They could give me any grade they wanted. It didn't matter.

The queasy feeling came back.

Lunch. I must need lunch.

So I made myself a sandwich and milk. I ate an apple imported from some place where the sun was shining. I felt full but no better. It was like I was still swallowing those candies.

What was my problem? I had everything a kid would want. Guaranteed straight As, guaranteed college, even a guaranteed job. And I didn't have to do anything for it but lose a few games now and then. Me, I'd win no matter what. Nothing I did mattered.

Nothing I do matters.

That was it. Nothing I did made any difference. The vampires had everything they wanted from me. All they needed were a few gadje to play in the water for them. That let them go up and down their marble halls in their quiet way, doing those incredible homework assignments, doing whatever they wanted in their school, while a few of us gave them the screen that let them do it. What they gave in return was nothing to them. They despised us.

They might not be sucking our blood, but they were sucking our pride.

Maybe that deal was good enough for Brian Blatt and good old Coach Underskinker, but it wasn't good enough for me. Tomorrow I was going back to that school, and I was going to find some way to pass for real. And I was going to play water polo to win, even if nobody else on the team did.

A few minutes later, Mom came home. Her nose was red from the cold and her breath was steaming.

"Are you feeling better, Cody?" she asked.

"I'm great," I said. "Have we got any Mozart CDs?"

MS. SHADWELL
DE-LYCANTHROPIZES

Of course, I still couldn't do the assignments. I listened to something by Mozart called *Eine Kleine Nachtmusik,* which means "a little night music" in English, and all I heard was a mess of notes. I listened two more times, and I heard them again.

Finally, I looked Mozart up in the encyclopedia and on the Web. Then I wrote:

Wolfgang Amadeus Mozart was born in 1756 and died in 1791. In between he wrote hundreds of musical compositions, including Eine Kleine Nachtmusik. *It has literally thousands of musical notes and a Köchel number of 525.*

I do not know what a Köchel number is, but I hope it is part of the answer to this question. Even if it isn't, please give me a real grade, Mr. Mach. I don't want your fake As.

Then I tried science.

The star Betelgeuse is, as we learned in class, a red giant four hundred to six hundred light-years from Earth. Someday it will explode. Four hundred to six hundred years after that, the first radiation from it will arrive here. No one can say exactly how much, or what will happen, but it could be bad for life on Earth.

You told us to look up the Van Allen Radiation Belts, which I did. They are belts of radioactive material in orbit around Earth that are trapped by our magnetic field. I don't know what they have to do with this question, but please give me a real grade, Ms. Vukovitch. I don't want one of your fake As just because I'm a gadje.

Social studies was easy. I just got a piece of beef jerky to take to school.

Dear Mr. Gibbon. Sorry I was absent. Here is some salted food. Please grade it the way you would a jenti piece of beef jerky. I don't want a fake A.

By now it was eleven o'clock. Mom and Dad were in bed. I didn't have any homework for English, but I wanted to get started on something anyway.

I'd never thought about writing before. How did people do it? Did they just sit down and start writing? How did they know when to stop? Where did they get their ideas?

That was what I needed, an idea. I thought about all the books I'd read. But they'd already been written. I thought about the things I'd heard about, seen on TV, or imagined. None of it gave me any ideas.

Finally, at 11:05, I decided to write an epic. Shadwell liked epics. Besides, an epic was poetry, and that meant the lines were shorter than in a regular story. That was a good reason to write one.

I got a clean sheet of paper and wrote.

The.

That was as far as I could get. The Epic of The. I just stared at that piece of paper until Dad got up and told me to go to bed.

Well, it wasn't due for another seventeen weeks. By that time, I'd have the rest of it filled in.

My teachers looked a little shocked when I turned in my homework the next day. As for the kids, they all looked at me like I was some kind of large bug they'd never seen before. They kept eyeing my cheek, which was funny because Ileana's mark was gone, as far as I could tell. Maybe vampires could still see it. A couple of times I caught people whispering the words *Ileana Antonescu* and *stoker*.

As far as Ileana went, she seemed not to see me at all, not even at lunch—I mean dinner. And as soon as she was done, she got up from her place at the table and disappeared.

I did get a smile and a "Hi" from Justin. I had the feeling he was waiting to see if I wanted to be friends. I wasn't sure about that, so I just said "Hey" back to him.

I didn't see Gregor or any of his gang except once on the stairs. They were coming down from the top floor, which meant they were at least juniors. If they saw me, they didn't give any sign of it.

When I got to water polo, the guys on the team

started chanting "sto-ker, sto-ker, sto-ker, sto-ker," and Brian shouted, "Hey, here comes a private supply."

It wasn't hard to get what he meant by private supply, but I couldn't figure out *stoker*. I wasn't going to ask these guys, though. I wasn't that dumb.

Underskinker came out from his office with a can of Old Aroostook in his hand and stared at us like he was surprised we were there.

Finally, he said, "Okay. We gadda team again. You punks get inna wadduh."

Groaning, the other guys jumped into the pool.

"Hey, Coach," said the semiweasel with red hair, "where's the ball?"

"Shudup, Lapierre," Underskinker said. "Just swim around till I tell yuh to stop." And he turned to go.

"Coach, I have some questions," I said.

Underskinker stopped, turned around, and pondered my statement. Finally he said, "Whud?"

"Like, what's our schedule of games?" I said.

"It's posted inna office," he said. "Look id up an' don' bodduh me." He rotated himself back toward the locker room and his beer supply.

"Well, when's our next game, then?" I called after him.

"Look id up," Underskinker said. "I ain't got time to tell yuh stupid punks everyting."

"I know when it is, I know when it is," Lapierre said, jumping up and down and waving his hand like a little kid. "It's next Tuesday after school, isn't it, Coach? Isn't it? Huh? Huh? Isn't it?"

"Whudevuh," Underskinker replied.

But I had another question.

"Coach, does this team have a name?"

He turned around so fast he almost fell over.

"Who dudn't know duh name of dis team?" he bellowed.

"Please, sir, nobody's told me," I said.

"Ellison, you stupid punk, we got duh same name as every udduh team at dis school," Underskinker said. "Tell 'im whud it is, punks."

Lapierre scratched his head and turned to Brian Blatt. "Do you remember?" he asked.

"Hey, man, you're the one who's supposed to remember the team name," Brian said. "I can't do it all."

A kid who looked like a box turtle spoke up. "It's Guns N' Roses, ain't it?"

"That's a rock group, Tracy, we're a team," Lapierre said.

"Oh, yeah," Tracy said, as if he was making a huge discovery. "Now I remember."

"I still think it's a cool name," said the fifth kid, who was as thin and mean-looking as a barracuda. "Let's be Guns N' Roses."

"You dumb, stupid, dumb, stupid, stupid dumb punks," Underskinker roared. "We're duh Impalers. You got dat?"

"Thanks, Coach," I said. "By the way, I think my name is Elliot. I'll ask when I get home."

Two guys laughed. One had blue eyes and acne scars like the craters on the dark side of the moon. The other was small and soft-looking.

"You. Elliot, Pyrek, Falbo. Gimme laps," Underskinker said, and headed for his office.

"Hey, Falbo," said the blue-eyed kid with acne scars, "give me some laps."

Falbo, the soft-looking little guy, said something about where Pyrek could get his laps, and everyone laughed again.

We all hung on the side of the pool for a few minutes and enjoyed the feeling of having yanked Underskinker's chain. I wondered if this meant I was going to start being one of the group.

Then the barracuda said, "You know, stoker, this was a real good team before you showed up."

"I can see that," I said, like what he'd said hadn't hurt.

He slid up out of the pool like a snake, tiptoed over to the locker room, and looked in.

Then he turned back and gave a thumbs-up.

"All right, Barzini," Lapierre said.

"Shut up," Barzini told him. "You wanna wake him?"

Everyone else got out of the pool, and after a minute I did, too. I wanted to swim by myself for a while, but even more I wanted to find Justin and ask him what a stoker was.

A lot of kids hung around the student union after classes. It wasn't hard to find someone who could tell me where he was.

"He works in the library on Friday afternoons, if I am not mistaken," a jenti kid named Anatol who was in my English class told me. "Do you know where that is, stoker?"

"I can find it," I said.

Actually, you couldn't miss the library. It was at the opposite end of the campus from the student union, and it was huge. It had two big wings extending out from an entrance that looked like a Roman temple. Over the door it said THE CHIEF GLORY OF EVERY PEOPLE RESIDES IN ITS AUTHORS.

The place was empty. I guessed even vampire kids didn't hang around a library on Friday afternoon. But I heard some soft noises from the left wing, so I went that way.

There was Justin with a wooden cart loaded with books, sticking them carefully onto the shelves.

He looked surprised to see me and maybe even embarrassed.

"Oh, hi, Cody," he said kind of loudly for a library. "Just a minute. Ms. Shadwell, someone's here."

Suddenly, around the corner of the shelves came a rat. And right behind it, running flat out, came a huge red wolf, snarling.

I screamed and jumped, but the wolf dashed past me and out of sight, after the rat.

Justin blushed. "That's Ms. Shadwell," he said. "I guess she'll be out in a minute, soon as she gets her clothes on."

There was a shriek from the rat, a snap of jaws, and a growl that rattled the bookshelves. Or maybe it just rattled me.

A raspy growl said, "Xhi—exxkooz—me. I—ee—rixt—xere."

I heard some thumps and rustles. In a few minutes I saw a big red-haired woman walking toward me with a huge white grin and her paw—I mean hand—stretched out.

"Hello," she said in a much nicer but really powerful voice. "You must be the new gadje in my husband's English class. Welcome, Master Cody."

"How do you do, ma'am," I said, being as polite as I could.

"Sorry about the wolf just now," she went on. "I've been trying to catch that rat for a week, and that's a lot easier to do if you're a wolf."

"Sounded like you got him, Ms. Shadwell," said Justin.

Ms. Shadwell licked her lips.

"That's the last book he'll ever gnaw," she said.

My stomach did a push-up.

"Now, how can I help you, Master Cody?" Ms. Shadwell said.

"Oh, I just came to ask Justin something," I said, trying not to think about the fact that I was face to face with a werewolf.

"Fine," she said, smiling more widely. "I'll be over at the desk if you want anything. Just ask. I *love* to help people find things."

"Thank you, ma'am."

As soon as she was out of earshot, I said, "My God, Justin, why didn't you tell me there were werewolves here?"

"Werewolves? There's no such thing," Justin said. "Not as far as I know, anyway. Ms. Shadwell's just a good lycanthropist."

"Come on, you know I don't know what that means."

"Just means she can turn herself into a wolf when she wants to," Justin said. "A lot of us can."

"I thought vampires—I mean jenti—turned into bats," I said. "Hey, can you turn yourself into anything?"

"Well, it's complicated," Justin said. "See, when you turn yourself into anything else, your weight and mass stay just the same. So no one could actually turn into a bat. I mean, what would be the point? A hundred-and-fifty-pound bat couldn't even fly. Now, some of us can turn ourselves into something kind of like a bat."

"But bigger, right?" I asked.

"A lot bigger." Justin was concentrating real hard on his books, avoiding my eyes. "Anyway, that's why a lot of us prefer wolves. It's more comfortable."

"Yeah, I guess I can see that," I said. I had an image of Justin flapping over New Sodom by the light of a full moon. "So—which do you prefer?"

"Well, it takes a lot of practice," Justin said. "And talent. Not all of us can do it."

"That's too bad."

Justin shrugged. "Doesn't matter a lot. In the old days, turning into a wolf or a giant bat thing was a good way to get away from your enemies. Nowadays we don't need it so much. My father was real good at it, though. Sometimes he had a wingspan of forty-five feet."

"Wow!"

"So what did you want to ask me?" Justin said.

"I want to know what a stoker is."

Justin nodded. "Somebody calling you that?"

"Just about everyone, I think."

"It's an insult," Justin said, sighing. "Try not to think

about it. It's not true, anyway. It's just 'cause you helped me Wednesday."

"But what is it?"

"Ever hear of a book called *Dracula*?" Justin asked.

"Sure. Everyone has," I said.

"Well, *Dracula* was written by a man called Bram Stoker," Justin said. "He met some jenti when he was traveling in Europe. And in America. He came here six times. One of my grandfathers talked to him. He seemed real friendly, real nice. Some of us told him some things about what it's like to be jenti. He took what we told him and wrote that damn book. Twisted everything we said. Ever since then, whenever a gadje makes friends with a jenti, somebody's going to say that the gadje's a stoker. There's only one worse thing we can call you."

"What's that?"

"A bram. Means you've gone and hurt the jenti in some way. And that's very bad if it happens. Word gets around you're a bram, somebody's going to get you for it."

"And when you say 'get'—" I began.

"I mean what you think I mean," Justin said. "Anyway, practically everything in *Dracula* is at least half a lie. And there was a lot of stuff he could have put in that he left out—the good stuff about us."

"Who got Stoker himself?" I asked.

"Nobody," Justin said. "Plenty of us wanted to, but he had Dracula's mark on him, and Dracula said no. Said it was his fault for trusting Stoker in the first place, and the best thing to do was let the whole thing die down naturally. You can see how well that's worked out."

"Wait a minute," I said. "Do you mean Dracula was real?"

Justin gave me a funny look. "Sure."

"So do you think I'm a stoker?" I asked.

"Nope. I think you're folks," Justin said.

"Which means?"

"Folks are gadje you can trust," Justin said.

All of a sudden I decided I liked Justin a lot.

"When do you get off?" I asked.

Justin looked at his watch. "Fifteen minutes."

"Want to hang out?"

"Sure," Justin said, giving me one of his weak little smiles.

"I'm going to take a look around," I said. "See you in a few."

"Right," Justin said.

The library was like everything else at Vlad Dracul— rich. Floor-to-ceiling bookshelves, computers every-where, armchairs, big tables, individual desks. The lights were warm and the carpets were thick. I couldn't hear the sound of my own footsteps.

There were big gold-lettered signs above the alcoves that ran along the walls: HISTORY. GEOLOGY. AMERICAN LIT-ERATURE. Then I came to the last one: DRACULA.

Every book inside was a copy of *Dracula*. Shelves and shelves of it in English, but there was a section that had it in other languages, too. *Every* other language, it seemed like.

"Are you finding everything you need?" asked Ms. Shadwell, coming up behind me.

"Oh, just browsing," I said. "Why do you have so many copies of one book?"

"It's required reading for every student at Vlad Dracul," Ms. Shadwell said. "You get it in fifth grade, eighth grade, and high school, just like American history."

"Maybe I should read it now, then," I said. I was trying to score a couple of points with her.

Ms. Shadwell acted like I'd just given her a Cadillac. "Wonderful!" she said. "Here, try this edition. No, this one. It's got very good notes. Or maybe this one; it's got a really great typeface."

She went on throwing *Dracula*s at me until my arms were full.

"Thanks," I said. "I guess I'll take this one." I set them down on a shelf and pulled one out of the stack like I'd been thinking it over.

"Can I help you find anything else?" she asked.

"No, thanks," I said. "I'm leaving with Justin."

"That's *great*," she practically shouted. "You come on back anytime, Master Cody."

Justin and I walked to his house. No limousine.

"I live close by," Justin said.

After a couple of blocks, we turned onto a long, narrow street where the trees arched over and their branches tangled together.

At the far end was a lopsided, teetery house that looked like it had been built onto about a hundred times in almost a hundred different ways. It went up and up, and on and on, and it looked like it had to be haunted on every floor. It was dark inside except for one light coming through a window by the front door.

"This is it," Justin said, letting me in.

I wondered, for just a second, if I'd ever see the outside world again.

As Justin pushed the door open, I saw a warm, low-ceilinged room. There was a place for us to take off our coats and boots before we went into it. As we did, a big clock on the wall quietly chimed four times.

From somewhere in the back, I heard beautiful piano playing. I recognized the tune. It was from *Eine Kleine Nachtmusik*.

"My mom teaches piano," Justin said. "Let's go upstairs. I'll introduce you later."

We went up a staircase so old it had waves in it like the ocean. It hardly creaked at all, though. I guess whoever had built it had known what they were doing.

"This is my place," Justin said. He opened a door on the second floor.

It was a little two-room apartment. One room was a regular bedroom, the other was full of fish tanks. That room had other stuff, too, like a telescope and a couple of good chairs and a table, but the rest was fish tanks. And the tanks only had one kind of fish.

"I raise angelfish," Justin said.

Everything looked old, comfortable, and used, even the fish.

"This is really cool," I said.

"You like fish?" Justin asked.

"I guess," I said. "I don't know much about them."

"I have all the kinds of angelfish there are," Justin said. "Blacks, marbles, golds. The regular silver and striped ones, of course. I sell the extras to pet stores. I've got customers as far away as Oregon."

I looked into the green-tinged water at all the fish, all almost exactly alike, swimming slowly up and down in their little worlds, silent and beautiful. For some reason, I thought of the kids at Vlad Dracul.

"Want to help me feed them?" Justin asked.

"Sure," I said.

There was a tiny refrigerator in one corner of the room. Inside it were lots of bags filled with limp brown worms as thin as hairs.

"Tubifex worms," Justin said. "They're like a dietary supplement."

He took one of the bags out and began to dump little clumps of the worms into the tanks. They floated at the top, a few in each bunch trying to wriggle out of the mass.

Every time Justin did that, the angelfish changed. Suddenly they were like hawks swooping on prey. They dashed to the worms so fast I couldn't even follow them. Then they began to yank the clumps apart. They inhaled the worms and went back for more.

"Here you go," Justin said, handing me my own bag. "That's all there is to it."

Feeling weird, I pulled out my first batch of tubifex worms. They were cold, slimy, and limp. They didn't move until I put them into the water. Then the angelfish were on them.

By the time we were finished, the angelfish in the first tanks were finished, too. They were cruising back and forth, searching for more worms. Looking into those tanks was like looking at some kind of living scientific chart: *Here are the fish going into feeding frenzy. Here are the fish in feeding frenzy. Here are the fish after feeding frenzy.*

One by one, in almost perfect order, the angelfish finished eating and settled down. Soon they were drifting up and down their tanks, like the kids in the halls at Vlad Dracul.

Vampires? What was I doing hanging out with vampires? Even if every word Justin said was true, no matter how nice they were if they liked you, didn't the time come when they had to drink blood? What happened then? What did Justin do? Or Ileana?

I must have looked pretty shocked because Justin asked, "Are you all right? You look kind of pale."

"Yeah, I'm fine," I said. "I just never fed fish before."

Justin said, "It's okay, Cody. It's not like that. Not anymore."

It was like he could read my mind. Was this another vampire power?

"If you want to know," Justin said quietly, "we mostly buy it. Pint at a time. It gets expensive, but we have to have it. It's like air to us."

"What happens if you don't get it?" I asked.

"We die."

"I always thought you guys were immortal," I said.

"Then where's my father?" Justin said bitterly. "We die, just like you do. We can live a lot longer; we're stronger and we can change shape, some of us, but if one of us gets hit by a truck or catches a disease, we'll die all right."

"Is that what happened to your father? If you want to tell me," I said.

Justin shrugged. "He was killed in a special forces operation overseas. He was part of a special night reconnaissance unit the army put together out of jenti volunteers. Very secret. So secret that he got shot down by his own side. They didn't know what he was. Of course, officially, it never happened."

"Oh, man, I'm sorry," I said, and I was.

"The army gives my mother survivor benefits," Justin said. "And we own our house. We've owned it for centuries. But that's about all we've got. There's not that much money in teaching piano lessons in New Sodom."

"I'd begun to think all you guys were rich," I said.

"Most of the jenti around here are," Justin said.

All of a sudden I realized something horrible.

"Justin, you've never had anybody over before, have you?"

After a minute, he said, "Nope. I mean, Ileana. We sort of grew up together. She used to live next door. Made mud pies and stuff. But you know how it is. We're not little kids anymore, and she's pretty busy after school these days."

Yeah, I knew how it was to have no friends. I thought of Justin going to school and scrounging for the grades I could have for nothing, coming home to a room full of fish for companionship. For the first time in a long time, I was feeling sorry for somebody besides myself.

"You know what, Justin?" I said. "You're pretty cool."

"Thanks," he said.

Below us the music stopped.

"Come on," he said. "I'll introduce you to my mom."

As we went down the stairs, we met Mrs. Warrener coming out of the piano room with her student.

It was Ileana.

"Oh, hello," Ileana said when she saw us. "This is a surprise."

"Justin's showing me his fish," I said. I was feeling a kind of tingle just looking at her.

"They are beautiful, are they not?" she said.

"And fierce," I said.

"Mom, this is Cody Elliot," Justin put in.

Mrs. Warrener took my hand in a strong, warm grip. "Thank you, Cody," she said. "Ileana told me about what happened at school this week."

Mrs. Warrener was really beautiful and her eyes were glowing as she looked at me.

"Oh. Well. No big deal," I mumbled.

"It was a bigger deal than you may realize," she said. "Would you and Ileana care to stay to dinner?"

I hesitated. I liked Justin all right, but what did vampires eat when they were at home and no gadje were watching?

"I will call my parents for permission," Ileana said. "It has been a long time since Justin and I spent any time together outside school."

If she was staying, I didn't care what I had to eat.

"I'll call, too," I said.

Mom gave me permission in nothing flat.

"Of course, darling. Have a good time," she said. "Just call when you need a ride home."

Ileana spoke to her folks in something that sounded

sort of like a combination of fountains rippling and gears grinding. I heard the words "Justin" and "Cody Elliot," and "okay . . . okay . . . okay."

She turned to us. "I can stay," she said.

Justin smiled.

ILLYRIA IN THE CELLAR

Want to know what vampires eat for dinner? Potato soup, salad, and apple pie. There wasn't a pint of blood in sight; not even a tubifex worm.

But the best part of dinner was the talking. Mrs. Warrener had this way of talking to us that made us talk to each other. She asked me a couple of questions about my old school, and that got Ileana and Justin interested, and they asked me things. They wanted to know about California, too. And Justin and Ileana had a lot of stories about Vlad Dracul. By the end of the pie, I felt like I was really beginning to know them.

After dinner Justin washed the dishes. I dried, and Ileana put them away. To keep up our strength, she said, Mrs. Warrener read to us from a book by a guy named James Thurber. He had a lot of crazy relatives out in Ohio, and the book was about them. The stories had titles like "The Car We Had to Push" and "The Night the Ghost Got In." I laughed so hard at that one that I dropped the salad bowl, which, luckily, was made of wood.

After we had finished, Ileana asked Justin, "Have you shown Cody Illyria yet?"

"Oh. No," Justin said. "Didn't think he'd be interested."

"It is still down there, yes?" Ieana asked.

"Oh, sure, I guess," Justin said.

"What is it?" I asked.

"Just this game we used to play," Justin said.

"It is the best game in the world," Ileana said. "It *is* a world, in fact. Let us show it to Cody."

"Well, I don't know," Justin said. "I haven't been down there in a while."

"Come on," I said. "If it's that good, I want to play it."

"It sounds like a fine idea to me," Mrs. Warrener added. "Why don't the three of you go down there for an hour, and I'll make chocolate for you when you come back up?"

"Okay then," Justin said. He walked over to the cellar door and flicked on a light. "But we don't have to stay if nobody's interested."

We went down more old steps, but these were made of stone. The cellar walls were stone, too. It was a huge place, with lots of shelves along the walls and mountains of old things piled up. There were big timbers holding up the floor above, and a stone arch halfway along. It looked like part of a castle.

But the floor was the best part. It was covered with bottles and boxes and all kinds of stuff that had been arranged to make toy cities. There were whole forests made of twigs set in lumps of clay, and mountains of plaster and chicken wire. There were rivers drawn with blue chalk and fields drawn with green chalk. And everywhere I looked I saw toy soldiers.

They weren't modern soldiers. They were hand-painted and made of metal. They rode horses and carried swords. Some of them were flat. Here and there were a few figures of princesses and ladies-in-waiting.

"Well, here it is," Justin said.

"Illyria," Ileana said happily.

She picked her way over to one of the towns at the far end of the cellar.

"This is my city," she said. "New Florence. City of poets, artists, and actors. No soldiers allowed."

I walked over and looked at it.

"This is the Rotunda," Ileana said, pointing to a big old cut-glass cake stand with a cover. "This is where the plays are performed and the poets recite."

"This is the cathedral," she went on, pointing to a carved wooden box with a blue bottle on top. "This is the hospital, this is the library, this is the coffeehouse, and that is the museum."

The buildings in Ileana's city were separated by parks and spaced around squares that flowed together. It was great, but something about it didn't make sense. The streets and squares were full of soldiers.

"I thought you said no soldiers allowed," I said.

"Look at them," Ileana replied. "Do they have weapons?"

They didn't. Every rifle, sword, and pistol had been broken off. Some of them were even missing arms or legs.

"No soldier is allowed into New Florence until he has lost his weapons," Ileana said.

"This is Anaxander," she said, handing me one of the armless ones, a cavalryman in a black uniform. "He is our greatest poet. Over there is his friend Vasco. He is the second-greatest poet but the greatest singer."

I noticed Vasco was short an arm, like Anaxander.

"All these men have given up war and found their true callings," Ileana told me.

"All these men have gotten broken," Justin said. "The good ones are in the other towns."

"Which one's yours?" I asked.

"That one," Justin said. "I call it Three Hills."

Three Hills was the biggest city in Illyria. It was built on three of Justin's chicken-wire mountains and the space between them. The big difference between it and the other towns was that it had a wall running all around the hills, with guard towers and cannons.

"This is totally cool," I said.

"We used to come down here every day," Ileana said. "Until I moved. But you have not kept developing it, Justin."

"I tried a couple of times," Justin said. "Wasn't much fun without you."

"Why is it called Illyria?" I asked.

"Because it is a beautiful name," Ileana said.

"Sounds kind of like yours," I said. "Ileana, Illyria."

"No, no," Ileana said. "It is a real place. Or was. It was a province of the Roman Empire. Also, Napoleon re-created it for a time. And Shakespeare wrote of it."

"But Shakespeare was just using the word," Justin said. "He didn't know anything about the real Illyria."

"That is why it is so perfect," Ileana said. "Because it is real and not real."

"How do you play?" I asked.

"We just made things up," Justin said.

"We made everything up," Ileana said. "We wrote their laws, their literature, and acted in their plays. We made their history happen. Then we wrote it. And there were things that happened to people. Adventures."

Justin was blushing. "It was just kid stuff," he said.

I looked at Illyria and wished it was real and I was there with Justin and Ileana.

"This is great," I said.

"Justin, let's show Cody how we used to do it," Ileana said.

"Well . . . ," Justin said.

"Please?" I said.

"Okay," he said. "That city over there is yours. It's called Palmyra, but you can change it if you want to."

Palmyra was a small place with only three big buildings and about a dozen soldiers. But it had a good harbor, and there was lots of room around it for new buildings.

"Palmyra is cool," I said.

By the time we had to stop, I had found some pressed-glass olive dishes and turned them into cargo ships. They were bringing in salt, and I was storing it in two rows of salt shakers that I was also using to line a long, straight road that I was building to connect Palmyra to New Florence.

I'd also started a park just beyond the new city hall, which was an old syrup can that looked like a log cabin.

Justin made a suburb for Three Hills. He took some walnut shells from the other towns and scattered them out a few feet from the wall.

"These are the houses for the people who don't want to live in Three Hills anymore because it has too many rules," he told us. "They're loyal but they want to relax more. They sell flowers and fruit to the city."

"There should be an inn or something," I said. "So people can come and visit their friends."

"Good idea," Justin said, and added an upside-down flowerpot.

"That's pretty big compared to the houses," I said.

"Well, maybe these people have a lot of friends," Justin said.

Ileana was having a debate in her council over whether or not to build a statue in front of the Rotunda. Her two poets were on opposite sides. They argued back and forth until she finally said to us, "My lords, we cannot decide this matter. What do you advise?"

So we got into it, with me on one side and Justin on the other, until Mrs. Warrener called us upstairs.

I didn't want to quit. It was the most fun I'd had since we came to Massachusetts.

Then I had a great idea.

"Did anyone ever write an epic about Illyria?" I asked.

"You mean a Shadwell-type epic?" Justin asked.

"Exactly."

"No," he said.

"Then would you mind if I did? I need to come up with something for English."

"No, you don't," Justin said. "Remember what I told you? You don't have to do anything."

"I remember," I said. "But I'm going to do it anyway. I turned in homework today and told all the teachers to give me real grades."

"No kidding?" Justin said.

"Do you think I can't do it?" I asked.

"It will be very difficult," Ileana said. "Gadje schools have not prepared you."

"Then I'll have to work harder," I said. "But I'm not going to fake it."

"Well," Justin said. "I guess I can help you if you want. I'm pretty good in school."

"Thanks," I said. "So it's okay if I write the epic?"

"You must write it," Ileana said. "I will tell you all the stories you want to hear."

Oh, boy. Shadwell was going to get the longest epic he'd ever seen.

While we were drinking our hot chocolate and talking about the epic, which I decided was going to be called *The Epic of Illyria*, Hamilton Antonescu came to pick up Ileana.

He was a neat-looking little man not much taller than she was. He had deep, friendly eyes and a gray mustache.

"How do you do?" he said, shaking my hand. Even

though he was a little guy, his grip was strong. All these vampires seemed to have muscles.

"I hope you're getting along at dear old Vlad all right," he said, smiling.

"I like it better than dear old Cotton Mather so far," I said. "Thanks for helping me to get in."

"Oh, you got yourself in," he said. "At most all I did was to speed up the process a little. May Ileana and I give you a ride home?"

"Sure, thanks," I said.

It was snowing again when we left, big feathery flakes that laid a frosting over the old snow and glistened in the branches of the trees. I decided it was beautiful. I also decided I was definitely in love with Ileana.

The funny thing about it was the way I felt. Scared and happy at the same time. I was glad she'd marked me. I had the feeling that somehow she'd made the night beautiful, as though she had made these huge snowflakes. Of course, she was a vampire. Maybe she had.

She sat beside me in the backseat, just taking in the snow and never saying a word. I wondered if she knew how I felt. I wondered if her father knew she had marked me.

Mr. Antonescu kept talking to me all the way to my house. I kept up my end, chatting about school while thinking about Ileana.

When we got home, I said, "Would you like to come in?"

I was proud of myself for remembering to ask, but Mr. Antonescu said, "Thank you, but I think we will not disturb your family so late. Good night, Cody. It was nice to meet you."

"Good night," Ileana said. "Remember to call if you need any stories from Illyria."

"I will. Promise," I said.

Mom and Dad were watching a DVD when I went in, one of those old movies that they liked, all black and white.

"Well, look who's here," Mom said, smiling. "Nice of you to take a little time off from your busy social life to join us."

"Have a good time?" Dad asked.

"The best," I said. "Mr. Antonescu brought me home."

"That was nice of Hamilton," Dad said.

"Did you ask him in?" Mom asked.

"Of course," I said. "I'm not a dumb kid."

"Certainly not," Mom agreed. "You're a verray parfit, gentil knyght."

"What?" I said.

Dad paused the DVD.

"I can see Mr. Bogart and Ms. Bacall will have to wait to pursue their relationship," he said. "All right, Beth, explain it to him."

"The verray parfit, gentil knyght was a character in *The Canterbury Tales,* by Geoffrey Chaucer," Mom said. "It's a collection of stories told by some travelers who are going to Canterbury Cathedral together. Each of them is supposed to tell two stories going and two coming back."

"Is it like an epic?" I asked.

"Something like that," she said.

So I asked, "Do we have a copy?"

"Two," Dad said. "One in modern English and one in the original Middle English."

"We got the modern one so your father could understand it," Mom said. "But the music's all in the original.

> "Whan that Aprille with his shoures sote
> The droghte of Marche hath perced to the rote,
> And bathed every veyne in swich licour,
> Of which vertu engendred is the flour;
> Whan Zephirus eek with his swete breeth
> Inspired hath in every holt and heeth
> The tendre croppes, and the yonge sonne
> Hath in the Ram his halfe cours y-ronne,
> And smale fowles maken melodye,
> That slepen al the night with open yë,
> (So priketh hem nature in hir corages):
> Than longen folk to goon on pilgrimages . . ."

Mom went on like that until she got to the knyght. I was reading along in the modern version:

> When April with its showers sweet
> The drought of March has pierced to the root
> And bathed every vein in such liquor
> Of which virtue engendered is the flower,
> When Zephyr also with his sweet breath
> Has inspired in every hold and heath
> Tender crops, and the young sun
> Has in the ram his course half run,

And little birds make melody
That sleep all night with open eye
(So Nature pricks them in their hearts):
Then folk long to go on pilgrimages . . .

It didn't make much more sense in the modern version.

"Where did you learn how to do that?" I said. "And why?"

"In college," Mom said, shrugging.

It's weird when your parents surprise you. And this was a thick book. More than three hundred pages.

"Can you do the whole thing?" I asked.

She laughed. "Just the Prologue," she said. "We all had to learn it."

This was amazing. Not only did my mom know some ancient poetry, but my dad had read the modern version of it. Plus, Geoffrey Chaucer had figured out a way to do what I wanted to do—write an epic made up of stories.

"I think I'll read these," I said.

Mom and Dad looked at each other.

"Three days at that school and he's reading Chaucer voluntarily," Dad said. "God bless Count Dracula."

"While his mother and father watch DVDs of old movies that were bad the first time," Mom said. "We're becoming unfit parents."

"Bogart and Bacall never made a bad movie," Dad said. "There may possibly be one with minor flaws."

"I'm going up to my room," I said. I took the two *Canterbury* books with me.

I put the books on my desk, feeling like a genius. I

would read Chaucer; then I'd be ready to write my own epic. Then Ileana would read it and see how great I was and fall in love with me.

I got into bed and lay there listening to the soft little hiss of the snow coming down in the parfit, gentil night.

GADJE GRADES

The next day, after breakfast, I got to work.

I set the two versions of *The Canterbury Tales* side by side and read them together. First I read a line in the modern English, then I read it in Chaucer's kind.

After an hour of that, I was ready to quit. It was like trying to run with my feet in two buckets of cement.

Plus, Chaucer wasn't that interesting. He had to introduce everybody who was going to tell the stories, and that took twenty-eight pages. And most of it didn't make sense. I knew what a knyght was, but what was a prioresse? Or a reve, or a maunciple? Only love kept me going to the end of the first part. By then it was lunchtime.

By the time I got back to work, I had some ideas of my own. My epic would have two poets in love with the same princess. Their names would be Anaxander and

Vasco. They would have a contest. Each of them would go to her palace to tell her stories, and the one who told the best one would get to marry her.

This was such a great idea that I bounced around in my chair while I was writing it down. All I needed now was the stories for them to tell, and Ileana had said she'd give me those.

I took the piece of paper I'd written *The* on a few nights before and added *Illyriad*. On the next line down I put *By Cody Elliot*.

I was so excited that I started writing my Prologue:

> *When in August with its days so hot*
> *The poets' horses in the dusty fields all trot,*
> *Then Anaxander and his friend Vasco*
> *Both to Ileana's castle go*
> *To tell her stories while she sits and listens*
> *And snow outside the windows glistens.*
> *Because they both want to marry her,*
> *But only one of them can carry her*
> *Away from her high tower,*
> *Where she lives every hour,*
> *To his own strong castle.*
> *And since they're friends, they cannot fight for her.*
> *They need some other way to compete for her.*
> *So they will entertain her*
> *And hope that then her brain hears*
> *The knight her heart prefers.*

No wonder Shadwell liked writing epics. I had nearly one page done already. I needed to make a few changes; I could see that. For one thing, the princess couldn't be named Ileana. But that was easy. My big problem was how to explain the snow glistening outside in the middle of August. But I didn't want to stop and figure that out now. I was rolling.

• • •

Monday morning started out pretty well. I had ten pages done on my epic. I had something done on each of my homework assignments. I was anxious to see what grades I'd gotten on the ones I'd already turned in, and I was looking forward to seeing Ileana and Justin. Plus, there was the natatorium to look forward to. Life wasn't easy, but it was starting to get interesting.

Then, about five minutes before Mom was going to take me to school, there was a knock on the door. When she opened it, a chauffeur was standing there.

"Master Cody?" he said.

Mom was in her old sweats and the chauffeur was dressed like a German general. She just stared. She hadn't seen any jenti close up before, and this guy was something. Tall, pale, long-faced, and his voice was oh so soft.

"Uh . . . yes. He lives here" was all she could say.

"See you, Mom," I said, sliding past her.

I turned and looked back as the chauffeur opened the car door for me. Mom was smiling and waving, but I could tell she was stunned.

I waved back, shouted, "Later," and got in, feeling good about how surprised she was.

This lasted about one second.

There were already four other kids in the car,

drinking coffee from the little espresso maker in the back. They were all older than me.

They looked me up and down, then went back to talking about whatever they had been talking about in that private language of theirs. Sometimes it sounded like grinding rocks. Sometimes it rippled like water over stones. In the middle of it, I heard two words I recognized: *gadje* and *stoker*.

"Just in case anybody in this car speaks English, I'm not a stoker," I said.

The four of them looked at me with blank faces, then went on talking. At least I didn't hear those words again.

But when I walked through those big gold doors, Ms. Prentiss was standing right there, waiting for me.

"Master Cody," she said, smiling. "Please come with me. Principal Horvath would like to speak with you."

"What did I do?" I asked.

"It's nothing like that, Master Cody," she said, smiling more widely and guiding me toward the office with her strong hand. Her nails had bright red polish and were really long.

Horvath was sitting in front of the fire. Charon was there, watching the door with his tail curled around his feet. So was every one of my teachers. There was one empty seat, between Horvath and Charon.

"Master Cody, come in," Horvath said, standing up and shaking my hand. "Please sit down."

So I sat down between the principal and his wolf.

"Master Cody, do you recall that on the day you came to us I told you that you might find our ways strange at first?" Horvath asked. "That I suggested you come to me with any questions you might have?"

"Yeah, I mean yes," I said.

The fire was casting shadows on the wall across the room. Mach's, Vukovitch's, Gibbon's, and Shadwell's looked like ghosts or monsters dancing. Charon's looked like a devil.

"Well, I wish you had done that," Horvath said, leaning forward. "From what your teachers tell me, you may have been getting information from sources that will lead you astray if you are not careful. That is why we are here. That is what we wish to prevent."

I looked around at their faces. They were all smiling at me except Charon.

"Please proceed, Mr. Mach," Horvath said.

Mach reached inside his coat and took out my homework assignment.

"It's the note you wrote at the bottom of this paper that concerns me," he said. "It sounds as though you think you have a guaranteed A in my class."

"That's what I heard," I said.

"I see. Well, it's a little more complicated than that," he said.

"If I may interject, we grade the whole student here, Master Cody," Mr. Horvath said. "As opposed to more ordinary schools where the assignments stand in isolation, apart from the total personality of the young scholar."

"But do you grade gadje and jenti kids the same way?" I asked.

Horvath raised his eyebrows. "Those terms are never used here," he said. "There is no need of them since, as I just explained to you, every student is treated as the individual he or she is."

"So if a jenti kid turned in my math assignment, what grade would he get?" I asked Mach.

"He'd get whatever grade he deserved based on his past performance and his background," Mach said.

"What grade did I get?" I asked.

"An A-minus," Mach said. "I think your work shows promise."

"How about my grade in science?" I asked Ms. Vukovitch.

"An A, of course," she purred, putting her fingers together. "After all, you were quite right; no one really knows what will happen when Betelgeuse goes nova. No other grade would have been possible."

"And how about social studies?" I said to Gibbon.

"A-plus," he said. "Not only did you fulfill the assignment, but it was the best piece of beef jerky I've ever had in my life. Thank you."

I turned to the last teacher in the circle. "You know what, Mr. Shadwell? Since you like epics so much, that's what I'm writing. I did ten pages this weekend, and I'll bet I can do three hundred easy by June."

"I'm sure whatever you do will be very acceptable," he said. "Please don't overexert yourself."

"Wait a minute," I said. "Last Wednesday you said you expected three hundred pages from us by the end of the year."

"A rough estimate," Shadwell said. "It's quite possible that the ten pages you have already written meet the assignment. Brevity is the soul of wit, you know. *Multum in parvo.* All of that."

"Every student brings something uniquely valuable to Vlad Dracul," Horvath said. "That is why each of you is here. In your case it is only fair to bear in mind that you have not had the advantages of an elementary education at our school. And yet you are talented in areas where we need talent. Water sports, for instance."

"But you don't have a real team," I said. "Those guys don't even want to get in the water. And Underskinker is a drunk."

Everyone laughed but Charon.

"I think you're mistaken there," Horvath said. "We have everything a team has—uniforms, a name, the natatorium. As for Mr. Underskinker, he's almost an institution here. Perhaps you just haven't seen him at his best yet."

"So what you're really telling me is that this school is just for jenti kids and as long as the gadje get in the water for you, you don't give a damn about us."

"I am telling you," Horvath said, putting his hand on my leg and squeezing a little, "that your grades are your teachers' concern. And that they are concerned about you. As we all are."

He stood up. So did everyone else. Their smiles came back on. Charon left the circle and went to lie down.

I was so mad I could barely talk. I hate to be lied to. It makes me crazy. And I was in a weird cave of a room where everyone was lying his head off except the wolf.

Horvath shook my hand again.

"I think—I hope—you understand us better now," he said. "But come to see me again anytime you are confused. Or at any other time. And remember, Master Cody, Vlad Dracul is not an ordinary school."

It was the first thing he'd told me that wasn't a lie.

Don't ask me what we covered in math or English or social studies that day. I was too mad to listen. And in gym I ended up doing a hundred jumping jacks because I forgot to stop when everyone else did.

When I got to dinner, Justin and Brian Blatt were already at the table, ignoring each other. But when I sat down, Brian took his face out of his plate and said, " 'S' up, stoker?"

That did it.

"Look, pizza face," I said. "Don't call me a stoker unless you want to finish that food without your front teeth."

Brian stood up and said something short, ugly, and as far as I know, impossible.

"I think I'd apologize for that if I were you," Justin said calmly.

"Who's gonna make me—you?"

"Well, if I have to, I suppose I could," Justin said. "What do you think?"

"Ooh, I'm so scared," Brian said. But he got up from the table without finishing his food. He even forgot to steal the rolls.

As soon as he was gone, Justin said, "That's the first time I've ever seen you act like a gadje."

"When you get treated like a gadje, maybe you start acting like one."

"What's the matter?" Justin said. "You've been looking mad all morning."

I took my math paper out of my backpack and showed it to him.

"What do you think you'd get on this if you turned it in?"

Justin looked at it closely.

"I'd guess I'd get an F."

"Can I see your paper?" I asked.

Justin took out his work. He had written pages of equations. There were even some sketches of music notes that were supposed to make his point, I guess. Mach had written all over his paper, and at the bottom was his grade: B—.

"Justin," I said, "you guys are different from us. You're stronger. You can fly. You can change shape. Are you smarter than we are, too?"

Justin thought it over.

"Don't think so," he said at last. "I think we just try harder. It's kind of expected."

Ileana sat down.

"You were in Mr. Horvath's office for a long time today," she said.

I told her what had happened.

"Would you care to show me some of your work?"

I showed her my assignments.

"Taking everything together, I think you are doing work on about a third-grade level," she said. "That puts you six years behind. It is a long way to come, but I am sure you can do it."

"Third grade," I said. "I'm dead."

When I got to water polo, Underskinker was standing on his hind legs near the diving board.

"You punks gadda game tomorrow," he announced. "Dat means two tings. First, when we play St. Biddulph's,

I want you punks to make it look like a game. No back floats or gettin' outta da pool before the game's over. Second, you gotta wear da caps. I don't care if you look stoopid in 'em. You look stoopid anyway. Tird, the backup team's gonna be here. Don't mess with 'em. Fourt . . ." Underskinker stopped talking. His forehead wrinkled up like a wet towel. For a minute his eyes almost focused. Finally he spoke. "Fourt is, don't forget what I told yuh."

He did one of his slow revolves and went back into his office.

As soon as he was gone, everyone else got out of the pool. I swam back and forth with my eyes closed, just enjoying the water.

The natatorium got quieter and quieter as the other guys left. Pretty soon there was nothing but the sound of me in the water, and that good, warm feeling came back. The feeling that I wasn't in Massachusetts, wasn't anywhere but right here, right now.

This feeling lasted until I opened my eyes.

When I did, there was Charon sitting by the pool. His big yellow eyes were staring straight at me.

"I think Underskinker is in his office," I told him. "I'd look for him under his desk if I were you."

Charon didn't move.

"Are you here for me?" I asked him.

Charon stood up.

"Okay, just a minute."

"Does Horvath want to see me again?" I asked as I climbed out of the pool.

Charon wagged low.

"That means no, right?" I said.

The tail wagged high.

"Okay, what is it then?"

His answer was to come right up to me. I took a step back. He followed.

What was this about? Was he going to attack me for mouthing off to Horvath? I took another step back. He followed me again.

"Is this about my grades?"

One wag very high.

Two more steps and I had my back against the wall.

"Listen," I began, "wait a minute. . . ."

Charon stood up on his hind legs and put his huge paws so heavily on my shoulders that I almost staggered.

He bent his head down and gave me a sloppy lick.

He dropped onto all fours and trotted to the door without looking back.

RULES OF THE GAME

The next day was Tuesday. That meant the Impalers had a game. Since we had never practiced, and I had never even learned what the rules were supposed to be, I was kind of curious to see what would happen.

At two-thirty, a small yellow bus drove up next to the natatorium. On the side of the bus it said ST. BIDDULPH'S EPISCOPAL SCHOOL EAST GEHENNA.

Fifteen guys got out. There were thirteen boys and two men. They walked to the natatorium in double file, almost like they were marching. They went in, keeping almost as quiet as jenti, and headed for the locker room.

Why so many? I wondered. The men were probably coaches, but why so many boys? Were some of them fans? No, all the boys had gym bags with the words ST. BIDDULPH'S SAINTS on the side.

I followed the Saints into the natatorium.

The pool was set up for the game. There were cages floating at either end to catch the ball, and white lines at the sides of the pool to mark the halfway point. There was a table at one side with four men sitting at it, and two more by the half-distance line and four more at the corners of the pool, all with whistles and little flags. It all looked very official.

I went into the locker room.

Underskinker was walking up and down the aisles, looking madder than I had ever seen him. He had a can of beer in his hand, of course, but he wasn't paying any attention to it.

Louis Lapierre saw him coming and shouted, "Coach, about this game—we don't have to get wet, do we?"

Underskinker crushed the can and beer sprayed out over his feet. Everyone on both teams laughed.

"You punks are all punks, you punks!" Underskinker shouted, and left.

Jason Barzini was putting on the little blue rubber bathing cap we had to wear.

"Hey, Barzini, you look cute in that," I said.

"Shut up, stoker, or you die," Master Barzini replied.

Brian Blatt said, "Come on, Barzini. Time for the real men to get out of here before the vamps show up." They followed the rest of the Impalers out to the pool.

I took a closer look at my own cap. Blue on the inside, white on the outside. Reversible. I turned it blue side out and put it on.

Around me the St. Biddulph's team were changing as quickly and quietly as they could.

"Say, how come there are so many of you and so few of us?" I asked.

None of them answered.

"So you're the Saints, huh?" I said.

No one answered me. They slipped on their white caps without looking left or right. In a minute, I was alone.

When I came out, the Impalers were in the deep end of the pool horsing around. The St. Biddulph's team had seven guys in the water and six along the back wall on a bench. I figured it out. They were replacements. They had replacements and we didn't. What a rip-off.

Then a line of jenti in team trunks and rubber caps came in.

Jenti in trunks? I figured it out in a minute. Our team needed a certain number of players, but there weren't enough gadjes. So to make everything look normal, Horvath had assigned six jenti guys to be on the team as replacements. They couldn't get into the water, of course. Replacements, only they would never replace anybody.

I saw Gregor at the head of the line. Behind him were Ilie, Vladimir, and Constantin. Then came one guy I didn't know. All tall, pale, fierce-looking guys. At the end of the line was Justin, like a period at the end of a sentence.

"Hey, man," I called.

"Hi," Justin said back.

All the guys from Saint Biddulph's ignored them, and

all the guys on our team except me laughed at them as they made their way to the bench.

I got out of the pool and went over to Justin. I stopped a couple of feet away to be careful not to drip on him.

"I didn't know you were on the team," I said.

"We're not. Mr. Horvath told us all to come down here and do this."

"But you guys never get in the water, right?" I said.

"Of course not. We can't," Justin said.

I wondered if Horvath knew about the fight last week and was putting Justin near Gregor as some kind of weird joke.

"Man, I would like to cream Horvath," I said. "That guy's a total phony."

"Who wouldn't? But that's the way it is." Justin shrugged.

"Well, maybe we can hang out after the game," I said.

"Maybe," Justin said.

The other jenti weren't even looking at me. They had their eyes straight ahead. They didn't even talk to each other. They were stiff, even for jenti, and I realized they were scared.

The judges were in position now with their little flags, so I got back in the water.

Brian Blatt and Jason Barzini were hitting each other, Louis Lapierre was floating on his face pretending to be dead, and Kelly Tracy was cannonballing by the diving board, trying to make a big enough splash to get the jenti guys wet. Milton Falbo was up on the diving board clapping his hands like a seal, and Pete Pyrek was hanging on the side of the pool, shouting to the jenti guys that the water was fine.

I didn't have the feeling that we were going to do real well against St. Biddulph's.

One of the refs blew his whistle and tossed the ball into the center of the pool. Instantly the St. Biddulph's guys went swimming toward it. One of them sent it sailing toward us. It came down right next to Lapierre.

Lapierre stared at it like it had just arrived from outer space.

"What is that thing?" he asked.

The others all gathered around it, shaking their heads.

"Don't know, never saw anything like that before," Kelly Tracy said.

"Blatt, pick up duh ball and throw it back," Underskinker shouted.

"What, this thing?" Brian shouted back. Then he turned to us and shrugged. "He says it's a ball."

"He ought to know, he's a coach," Milton Falbo said.

"He wants you to give it back to those guys over there," Pete Pyrek said.

"It must be theirs," Brian said. He took the ball, got out of the pool, and went over to the other side.

"Anybody lose this?" he asked the St. Biddulph's guys.

"Come on, Blatt, get back in duh wadduh," Underskinker bellowed. He looked like he wanted to hit Brian.

"Oh, okay," Brian said. He splashed into the water on the St. Biddulph's side.

"Not dat wadduh," Underskinker roared. "Dat wadduh ovuh dere. Dat's yer wadduh."

"Looks just like the other water over there, Coach," Brian said. But he got out and got back in on our side.

Back came the ball and splashed right beside Milton Falbo.

"Hey, this game's dangerous," he said.

"Yeah, he could have been killed," Kelly Tracy shouted.

"I'm gettin' out of here," Pete Pyrek said. He dived under the water and came up on the St. Biddulph's side.

"Can I be on your team?" he asked.

"Pyrek, get back in dat wadduh. Dat's your wadduh," Underskinker shouted.

"But, Coach, they're throwing things at us," Kelly Tracy said.

"Please let me be on your team," Pete Pyrek said. "Look. I got a hat," and he turned his bathing cap white side out.

"Hey, look, you guys. Mine's white on the inside, too," Brian Blatt said.

"So's mine," said Milton Falbo.

"Mine, too," said Kelly Tracy.

"Wow, so's mine," said Louis Lapierre.

Jason Barzini didn't say anything. He just turned his cap inside out. Then, on a signal from Brian, they all dived down and swam over to the St. Biddulph's guys.

The referees blew their whistles and the game stopped. The refs and coaches huddled. They knew they had to do something, but what? They were whispering, but I could hear Underskinker's voice saying "no way" and "penalties" and "personal foul" over and over. And, of course, "punks."

Finally, after a couple of minutes, the referees declared personal fouls on all the Impalers but me. The rest of the team got out of the water and headed for the chairs where the jenti guys were sitting.

"Hey, 'scuse us, it's our turn to sit down," Brian Blatt said to Justin.

"Yeah, replacements into *duh wadduh*," Pete Pyrek said.

Everyone on the bench but Justin looked at Gregor. Gregor sat looking straight ahead. Pyrek and Blatt kept shouting, "Replacements in duh wadduh, replacements in duh wadduh," until Gregor finally turned to Ilie and said, "Did you hear something?"

"Why, yes," said Ilie. "I believe I heard the sound of two meadowlarks. Spring must be coming."

"Meadowlarks," Gregor said, and closed his eyes. "Pretty little sound," he said, smiling.

All the jenti closed their eyes and smiled with him except Justin. Justin just kept looking at the pool, and at me.

That was a long thirty-five seconds. The Saints batted the ball back and forth among themselves a couple of times, then sent it over my head. I threw it back. They hit it off to one side and I swam over to get it. And threw it back. And back it came. And back I sent it. And so it went, with me getting angrier and more embarrassed as the thirty-five seconds went by.

When the penalty was over, the whistles blew and the Impalers got back in the water. The ball came high and slow right toward me. I made a fist and spiked it back over the line.

Immediately every whistle in the place went off.

"Penalty. Thirty-five seconds."

"Me? What'd I do?" I shouted at the judges.

"You spiked the ball, stoker," Jason Barzini said.

"Well, damn it, nobody told me," I exploded.

More whistles.

"Penalty. Thirty-five seconds."

Brian shook his head. "Profanity, man. I'm shocked."

I got out of the pool and went over and sat down near Justin.

"Is everybody here nuts?" I asked him.

"More or less, I guess," he answered.

Meanwhile, all the other Impalers were shouting, "Profanity, profanity. We don't want to be on a team with a guy who uses profanity." They splashed and held their ears. "Man, that offended us."

Then somebody must have given the signal, because they all dived at once and came up on the St. Biddulph's side again.

"Hey, we still want to be on your team," Pete Pyrek said.

"Yeah. You wouldn't use profanity, would you?" said Kelly Tracy.

"Don't be stupid, Tracy," Brian Blatt said. "These guys go to a school for saints."

"Oh, yeah," Tracy said. "I forgot."

If the Saints were grateful for their new teammates, they didn't show it. They kept shooting nervous looks at the jenti on the bench. They didn't even seem to notice the Impalers around them.

Meanwhile, Underskinker was walking back and forth along the side of the pool, shrieking, "Dat's not you punks's wadduh. *Dat's* you punks's wadduh ovuh dere."

"We don't like dat wadduh," Louis Lapierre shouted back. "It's got profanity in it."

Then my seventy seconds were up and I got back into the profanity—I mean the water.

Back came the ball, heading straight for me, once again. I slapped it back. Back it came, the same way. After a few more passes like that, I saw what the St. Biddulph's guys were doing. They were aiming the ball at me, trying to make it look like a real game.

As for the Impalers, they were cheering every time the ball came their way but staying clear of it. The St. Biddulph's guys played around them like they weren't there.

Meanwhile, I was getting really thrashed, trying to swim and hit the ball back every time. I was almost grateful when Jason Barzini suddenly came to life, slapped the ball before a St. Biddulph's player could get it, and sent it skimming into the net behind me.

Instantly flags went up and the judges declared the game over, 1–0 St. Biddulph's.

Everyone got out of the water but me. I swam over to the edge of the pool and hung there, breathing hard and feeling angry and confused. What the hell, weren't these so-called grown-ups supposed to enforce the rules they made up? Even I knew this game wasn't half over.

But here was everybody walking around, heading back to the showers, Underskinker and the St. Biddulph's coach shaking hands, and the judges and refs packing up their flags and stuff as if they hadn't just been part of a scam.

Then I looked up into the bleachers and saw Horvath

and Charon sitting there, Horvath with this cynical grin on his face and Charon looking disgusted, if a timber wolf can look disgusted.

The jenti guys just went on sitting on the bench. They were waiting for the gadje to leave before they went into the locker room. Well, I wasn't ready to leave yet. I wanted to do something to get rid of the bad feelings. So, even though I was tired, I began to swim slowly, stopping to float, letting the water carry me. I closed my eyes.

I opened them again when my head brushed the side of the pool. It made me remember I was wearing that stupid cap. I took it off.

By now the Saints were hurrying out to their bus and the Impalers were drifting out of the locker room, slapping each others' butts and throwing high fives.

At a signal from Gregor, all the jenti got up and headed for the locker room. All but Justin, who came over to me.

"Well, that was your first game," he said.

"What is it about you guys and water?" I said. "I mean, you take baths, don't you?"

"Let's go someplace drier and I'll tell you," he said.

He backed up while I got out of the pool. When I had dripped off enough, we walked into the locker room together.

The jenti were getting dressed and getting out as fast as they could.

Gregor looked over at me.

"The water is the only place you are safe," he said.

"He's marked," Justin reminded him.

"I was talking to you," Gregor said.

He finished buttoning up his shirt and brushed past us, pushing with his door-width shoulders. I ran my fingers through my hair to collect some water and flicked it on his cheek.

"Good game, Gregor," I said as he brushed it away like it was poison. "Looking forward to the next one."

Then I stripped off my wet trunks. "Well, time to wring my suit out."

Gregor backed away and left.

"Who needs garlic and crosses?" I said without thinking. Then I looked at Justin. "Oh, man. I hope that wasn't anything insulting."

"Don't worry about it," Justin said. "Anyway, just so you know, my mother wears a cross and cooks with garlic. But watch where you wave that suit."

"Okay, so now tell me about you guys and water," I said, drying myself with my towel.

Justin sighed. "Nobody really knows how it works. And our doctors and biochemists have been trying to understand it for a long time. But it's got something to do with our ability to change shape. Water, too much of it, can dissolve us. We're raised with stories about not going near the water, and we're taught to take sponge baths. Anything we can do to limit our contact with it. We all grow up scared of it."

"But you can't change shape," I said. "Maybe it'd be safe for you."

"Wouldn't be a good idea to try to find out," Justin replied. "I admit, though, it looks like fun getting into that pool."

I thought about all the angelfish swimming in the

room in Justin's house. "But don't you ever have to dip an arm into one of your aquariums? Clean out the tanks?"

"Sure," Justin said. "And I wear rubber gloves when I do it. Anyway, we don't fall apart right away when we hit it. We're not made of sugar, you know. But if we fall in a pond or something and we don't get out pretty fast, we start to sort of . . . dissolve, like I said. It happens faster in flowing water. That's why there are all those stories that we can't cross rivers, or we can only cross oceans in coffins filled with dirt."

When we left the natatorium, the Impalers were waiting for us.

Brian Blatt pushed in between me and Justin. "Excuse us," he said. "We want to talk to this guy for a minute."

He stood in front of Justin while Jason Barzini grabbed my coat and shoved his face into mine. The rest of the team made a circle around us.

"You looked real cute today," he said. "Real cute playing all by yourself. Well, the next time you try it, you're gonna get hurt."

"What are you punks trying to prove?" I said, sounding like Underskinker all of a sudden. "That you can lose games? Anybody can do that. Why don't you at least try?"

"Look, these vamps got what they want from us," Barzini said. "We keep their school open for 'em. They got vamps comin' in from all over the world to go to school here. And we pay the taxes for it, us real people. And the only reason they even let us in is so they can stay open. It's a scam, us being here. Act like it, like we do."

"Hey, Barzini, the jenti pay taxes, too. Ever think of that?" I said. "They pay the taxes that keep you here."

"Shut up, " Barzini said, and shoved me.

The ice was slippery and I went down. The rest of the Impalers snickered.

I hooked one of my boots under Barzini's leg and flipped him down on his back.

Then I got up, while he called me names.

"You guys don't like it here, why don't you try real school?" I said. "I'll bet there's some openings in kindergarten."

They didn't try to stop me as I went back to Justin.

"Bye-bye," I said to Brian.

"You're gonna die," Jason Barzini called to my back.

THE ILLYRIAD

January went by. We played two more games, and they were a lot like the first one. The only guy who even tried to do it right was me, and we only played until the other team scored. There were always different jenti sitting on the bench behind us. No matter how many of the Impalers got penalty time-outs, they never replaced us, and no one seemed to notice.

I was still a little worried about what the Impalers might try to do to me, but all they actually did after that day in the snow was to stop talking to me. Since they had never really started, this was no big deal. Barzini, I decided, was all mouth.

I was a little more worried about Gregor and his bunch. There were days when it seemed like every time I turned around they'd be looking at me from across the dining hall or from the top of a staircase. Maybe they were checking to make sure I was still marked. But nothing happened with them, either.

I got more impossible homework assignments. The fake As kept coming, but I ignored them. I got in the habit of going over to Justin's after school to work on stuff. I wouldn't say I did great, but I did better with his help. Sometimes I even almost understood what I was supposed to be doing. I really enjoyed sitting in the little room on the second floor where Justin fixed up a sort of office for us, with books and shelves and a terminal and all the stuff he needed to work at home. It even had a huge old desk, called a partners' desk, where we sat across from each other and did our work while the piano music came up the stairs.

It was crowded in that little room, but we managed to find space for Ileana when she came by, which she started to do once or twice a week.

The best days were Fridays, when we'd all end up down in Illyria. Palmyra was growing, and the road to New Florence was finished. Justin was putting in more suburbs around Three Hills. Ileana said the latest argument between Anaxander and Vasco was whether a play should have three acts or five.

"But when am I going to see the epic you are writing about Illyria?" she asked me every time we played.

"When it's finished," I'd say. "But I'm stuck for ideas."

Then she'd say something like "How can anyone be stuck for ideas? Illyria is where ideas begin," and she'd tell us another story about one of her characters while Justin and I asked questions or made suggestions for it. I don't know if this was how Chaucer did it, but it worked for me.

I was glad I had that epic. It was one thing I could do where I didn't need Justin to hold my hand. I wasn't even really stuck for ideas; I just liked Ileana's better than mine. But I used both. Evenings or Sundays I'd just sit down in my room and start writing, and the pages piled up. It looked like there was even a good chance I might have more than three hundred. I thought about how it would be, the day I handed it in to Shadwell. Would mine be the thickest one in the class? What would he say if it was? What would I say to him?

Hope you like it, Mr. Shadwell. It's somewhat Chaucerian. Or, *I'm afraid I went a bit over three hundred pages on this one.*

But better than that was imagining what Ileana might say. That was what I was really hoping, that she'd read it and see how much she meant to me.

I wouldn't say I was totally in love with Ileana. Not exactly. I just wanted to spend every minute I could with her. And I was beginning to think she felt the same way. Not that she said anything to make me think so. It was just a few little things, like not moving around Illyria so that we were always on opposite sides of it, or letting me push my cup of cocoa so that it touched hers by accident. When the epic was finished, I thought, things would be different.

Then came February the fourteenth.

February the fourteenth should be written down in

history with the other great disasters, like the San Francisco Earthquake (April eighteenth), the crash of the *Hindenburg* (May sixth), and the Great Chicago Fire (October eighth). February the fourteenth is Valentine's Day. It was the day I read part of my epic to Ileana.

It wasn't my idea. I wanted to wait until it was finished. But one Friday afternoon in Illyria the three of us got to talking about Shadwell's class, and one thing led to another. Justin talked about the book he was writing on angelfish. Ileana was writing a novel and told us about that.

Then she said, "And how is your epic coming?"

"About two hundred pages," I said. Some of them were even written on both sides. "I've got eleven stories done, and I'm starting on the twelfth."

"I would love to hear some of it," she said.

She had said things like that before, but that day I happened to have part of it with me.

I'd brought it to school to type it because my own computer was acting weird.

"It's not ready yet," I said.

"Please," she said. "I have been telling you stories for it for weeks now. May we not hear something of what you have done?"

It's Valentine's Day. The girl I love wants to hear something I've written, which is about love.

Justin was there, but he was cool. He'd probably be around whenever I read it. I decided I'd better do what she wanted. Besides, maybe—you know—maybe it was time.

So I went and got it.

On my way up the stairs, I remembered one little detail that I couldn't believe I had forgotten. My epic still had Ileana's name in it.

Quick. What's a name that's got the same rhythm as Ileana but doesn't sound like it?

All the way up the stairs I was trying to think of one, and I couldn't. On the way back down the stairs, I couldn't think of names at all. Imagine not being able to think of Jane, or Kathy, or Jennifer. But I couldn't. Total fear made me totally stupid.

When I got back to the basement, I took my pages, stood up by my city, and said, "This is a place where my heroine asks the heroes to tell her a story that is not about somebody else. It's supposed to be about something real that happened to each one of them."

Ileana folded her legs under her and leaned toward me with her hand under her chin. Justin sat on a crate with his back against the wall.

A name, a name, I have to have a name.

And then one came. A name so bad that it was the only thing I could think of that was worse than using Ileana's. But it *was* the only thing I could think of. Buffy. There was no way out. So I started.

> "So Vasco turns to Anaxander,
> Who's smiling like a salamander,
> And says to him, 'Now tell another story.
> Make this one about me, and make it true.
> And I will do the same for you.'
> And Anaxander says, 'I will.'
> And says to . . . Buffy, 'My friend is quite heroic

>   *In his way, but he would never tell you what I'm*
>   *going to say.'"*

Ileana was just sitting there with a little smile on her face. I went on.

> "One time Vasco heard there was a bandit with a
>   golden sword,
> Which he had robbed from some dead king
> Who long ago had lost the thing in battle,
> And Vasco wanted to return it to the king's
>   descendants,
> Who still mourned its loss
> And wanted it brought back at any cost.
> So Vasco made a pilgrimage to find the bandit's lair.
> He dressed up like a maunciple to catch
>   him unaware,
> And rode a hundred days until he came to that far
>   place
> Where the bandits had their cave. And then our
>   Vasco gave
> The bandits money for his stay that night. And
>   knew that they
> Would try to kill him and there'd be a fight."

Ileana wasn't smiling now. She was frowning. The hand that was under her chin curled over her mouth.

> "That night, as Vasco feigned his sleep,
> The bandits to his bed did creep.
> But as the largest raised a club to smash his skull,

Vasco rolled away with all his skill,
And threw his blanket over the bandit's head
And smothered him until he fell down dead.
The bandit chief with mighty roar did charge
And near stomped Vasco flat, for he was large,
And twenty other bandits joined in,
And Vasco's future started looking grim.
But he smote the club upon the bandit chief
And brought all of the bandits' plans to grief.
The bandit chief sank down upon one knee
And uttered, 'Vasco, thou hast ruined me!'
'Our chief does die,' the other bandits cried,
And turned and tried to get outside.
But with their backs all turned they could make no
      defense,
For fear of Vasco had destroyed their common sense.
So with club and the dead king's sword
He cut the bandits down within the cave and went
      homeward."

I was just about to say, "It'll be longer when I finish
it," when Ileana interrupted me.

She laughed. She laughed and laughed. She rolled on
her back and kicked her feet against the floor and went
on laughing.

Justin smiled at me. "Pretty good," he chuckled. "I
didn't get it at first."

"Neither did I," Ileana gasped. "For a minute, I
thought you were making fun of them, and I began to get
angry. Then I saw that you were making fun *with* them.
That is quite wonderful, having Vasco signal his friend to

amuse the princess with a silly story, and then having Anaxander tell it in such clumsy words."

"I like the part where Vasco suddenly grows his arm back so he can smother the bandit," Justin said.

Oh, God. I forgot these guys only have one arm apiece.

"Is there any more?" Ileana asked.

"Uh . . . no," I said, feeling like the ground was falling out from under me.

"That is a shame," Ileana said. "I never thought of Vasco and Anaxander as having senses of humor. But of course they would. You are giving something new to Illyria. Irony."

I could feel my face getting hot. She thought it was funny. It wasn't funny; it was an epic. But if she thought it was funny, if Justin thought it was funny . . . I looked at my pages again.

"I'm not quite sure if Shadwell covered irony in class," I said, holding my voice as steady as I could.

"It's like saying a thing one way and meaning it another," Justin said. "For a joke, or to be sarcastic."

Irony? This wasn't supposed to be irony. I'd thought it was good. Even worse, my whole epic was like this. The whole impossible thing of trying to make it at Vlad Dracul hit me all at once, and I felt like I was falling down a well.

Then Ileana got up and came over.

"It was hard for you to read this to us, I can tell," she said. "Thank you."

And she gave me a quick hug.

Oh, man.

Do you know what it feels like to find out something

you were proud of is a piece of junk? And then to be praised for it by mistake? And to know that the girl you were hoping to impress thinks it's a joke and is impressed for the wrong reason? If you don't, I hope you never find out.

"Next time I hope you will bring one of the serious parts," Ileana said.

"Well," I said, "I don't know about that."

I think Ileana and Justin wondered why I was so quiet the rest of the afternoon.

WHAT TO GET FOR
THE VAMPIRE WHO HAS
EVERYTHING

I was sitting in the dining hall with Justin the Monday after my epic disaster. It was another bleak, ugly day outside and exactly matched how I felt.

The worst thing about reading my lousy, no-good poetry to Ileana was that now she thought I was gold dust. I was sure that if I asked her to go out with me, she'd say yes. But how could I do that, knowing she'd be saying yes because she thought I was writing a great—well, a good—poem about her favorite place?

Ileana sat down.

"I am angry with you," she said.

"Huh? What'd I do?" I asked.

"I passed you a note in mathematics, a perfect note, and the first gadje thing I have ever done in my life, and you did not even notice it," she said.

"I'm sorry," I said. "I've got a lot on my mind."

Like what happens when you find out that I can't write poetry. That I can't even tell good from bad. That the joke's on you for thinking I can, and on me for ever thinking I could.

"That is all right." Ileana laughed. "Here, I have an extra one."

She took a little golden envelope out of her purse.

"Should I open it now?" I asked.

"If you like," she said.

Inside was a pale square card covered with fancy printing:

Ileana Antonescu requests the pleasure of your presence
on the occasion of her Fifteenth Birthday celebration
at two of the clock on Saturday, the Seventh of March.
Dress Formal.

Below were her address and phone number and the letters RSVP.

"Great," I said. "I'll be there."

"I am looking forward to it," Ileana said, and smiled at me. "By the way, how is the epic coming?"

"Oh. It's coming," I said, and changed the subject.

Now I had two worries—what Ileana would think if she found out what a lump of tubifex worms my poem really was, and what to get her for her birthday.

Justin was absolutely no help when I asked him.

"That's easy." He smiled at me. "Just give her one of the stories from your epic. It'd be the best thing you could do for her. I'll bet it'll be her favorite present."

"Uh," I said. "What are you getting her?"

"Don't know," he said. "It'll have to be something small."

"Well, what does she like?" I asked. "Everybody's got favorite things."

Justin nodded. "She's got a lot of those," he agreed. "Most of them aren't really things to buy, though. She likes stars. Clouds, the big puffy ones. Oak trees. She told me once she loves the sound of seagulls more than music. And she loves music a lot."

"Maybe I could get her some CDs," I said.

"Maybe." Justin shrugged. "But you asked me what she'd like from you, and I told you."

My dad was as helpful as usual.

"Cash," Dad said. "If she's Antonescu's daughter, any sum larger than a nickel will make her break down and weep for joy."

Mom tried, at least.

"Books always show a great deal of regard," she said. "They show a man values a woman for her mind."

"That's cool," I said. "Except that Ileana has probably read an entire library. It's amazing how much she knows."

"It's hard to go wrong with a good book of poetry," Mom said.

Poetry again. Why were people so hung up on poetry? Okay, why were *women* so hung up on it? But I figured Mom was probably right. Anyway, I didn't have any ideas of my own.

The next weekend, I went to the biggest bookstore around. Actually, there were two big bookstores in New Sodom. One was one of those big chain stores. Quite a few people were going in and out, and the lot was full of cars. Ordinary cars. On the next block was a big old-fashioned building of stone with a window so dark you could hardly see through it. Painted on it in gold leaf was AURARI'S FINE EDITIONS. EVERYTHING THE READER WILL REQUIRE.

I didn't need the exotic old cars in front to tell me whose bookstore was whose.

I knew I was supposed to go into the chain store. If I'd been buying for anybody else, I probably would have. But this was for Ileana. I went into Aurari's.

There were two floors. The upper one was a balcony that ran all around the room about fourteen feet up, and you could see the customers up there browsing through the ceiling-high bookcases under the dim, rich glow of the old-fashioned lights. The lower floor was even darker and had huge leather chairs in the center of the room.

In a corner of the ground floor they had about nine million poetry books, starting with Anonymous and ending with Yeats. They all looked alike to me—thin and expensive. I spent an hour going through them, and they all sounded alike to me, too. I didn't have a clue.

Finally, I turned away in disgust and started looking around the rest of the store. It had a lot of stuff besides books. There were globes, reading lights, bookends, even candy wrapped in gold paper.

On a table near the doors, I found a stack of books in leather covers with fancy designs burned into them. They even had little clasps to lock them with. There was one I really liked. It was red and covered with leaves.

I opened it. Inside, the book's pages were blank.

Hmm. At least I know she hasn't read this one.

I looked at the price. When my heart started beating again, I wondered how they could charge so much for a book that didn't even have words in it. I counted my money. If I didn't mind being broke for the next week, I could get it for her.

"May I be of any assistance whatever?" said a voice behind me.

I turned around and saw a jenti with rimless glasses and a black suit.

"Just this," I said.

"Very good," said the jenti. And I knew he meant "It's very good you are leaving."

Then I looked up, and I saw that all the customers on the second floor were staring down at me. But the ones on the ground floor wouldn't look my way at all.

"I understand there is quite an acceptable bookstore in the next block," said the jenti clerk as he made change out of a little wooden box. "In future, I would recommend that you shop there."

"Thanks a lot," I said, and left.

On the way home, I thought about Ileana and what she might put into the book. Maybe she would write her own poems. Maybe she would keep a diary in it. Maybe it would be full of stuff about me.

But something didn't feel right to me about that. It was like there was something the book needed before I could give it to her. Something I had to do.

Which did not make any sense.

On the way home, there was a bridge over a little creek. I leaned on the bridge railing and looked down.

Most of the creek's water was still locked up in ice, but a tiny trickle ran down the middle like a vein full of blood.

I remembered Justin and the day I'd met him. How frightened he'd been of that fast-flowing water. It gave me the urge to go down there and put my hand in the creek. Maybe I couldn't think as well as a jenti, maybe I'd never know as much, but there were some things I could do that none of them could.

Being very careful of Ileana's book, I slid down the bank and hunkered down at the edge of the ice.

The water looked happy to be moving so fast. Come to think of it, it probably was. It was going somewhere, unlike me. It would join up with a river, find the ocean, and who knew, maybe in time it would flow out of the Atlantic and into the Pacific and wash up on the California coast. I'd be here.

I put my hand in the water and held it there until it was numb. When I couldn't feel my fingers anymore, I walked downstream a little way.

The creek made a bend, dropped down a few feet, and made a tiny waterfall. The pool at the bottom of the fall was mostly ice, but there was one spot where the water hit that was still unfrozen. The clouds were reflected in it, jiggling as the water rippled.

Clouds. Ileana likes clouds.

A cold breeze blew down the creek, and the stiff, dead reeds moved. Something fluttered at their roots. A few seagull feathers.

I pulled one away from the frozen ground.

And she likes seagulls.

Now I knew what the book was missing. I had to

figure out a way to fill it with Ileana's favorite things. A book of clouds and seagulls and everything else Justin had told me she liked. I didn't know how I was going to do it, but I had a start. I was holding it in my frozen fingers.

How do you put clouds into a book? Here's what I did. I borrowed Dad's camera and went out in the backyard and shot a roll of film at the sky.

It took all morning, waiting for some clouds that looked halfway interesting, then shooting them three or four times as they moved. I'm no photographer, but even I know you can't count on one shot.

Then I went around the neighborhood looking for oak trees. When I found them, I moved the snow away and searched for golden brown leaves. Finally, I had enough to cover a solid page. I glued them down on a page in the middle of the book and sprayed them with lacquer for protection.

The seagull feathers I sort of arranged like a pair of wings at the beginning.

When the pictures came back from the developer, I took the best ones and trimmed them to fit onto a page between the other two, then glued them on. None of them were the kind of cloud Justin had said was Ileana's favorite, but taken all together, they looked pretty good.

What had me stumped was how to give her stars. Pictures wouldn't work. In the first place, it was cloudy all the time. In the second place, I knew that photographing stars doesn't work. Dad had tried it once when he first got his camera, and all that had come out were dim little points of light. I thought about using paper stars, but that seemed too much like fourth grade.

Then I thought maybe I could give her something that stars are made of, the way diamonds are made out of coal. So I asked Ms. Vukovitch.

"Stars are chiefly hydrogen, of course," she told me. "But they contain all the elements in trace amounts."

Great. A little bag of hydrogen stapled to the last page of her book. That'd be great for Ileana.

Her birthday was getting closer, and I was getting nowhere.

On the Monday before her party, I was sitting in the family room watching TV. Mom had gone out and Dad wasn't home, so I was channel surfing, which they hate and won't let me do. They won't get me my own set, either, which would solve the problem.

Anyway, I flipped past one of those psychic hot line ads, and there they were above the 800 number—stars.

Stars. Psychic. Astrology.

I called Justin.

"Hey, Justin, was Ileana born here in New Sodom?" I asked.

"Sure."

"And is the seventh really her birthday?"

"Nope. It's the sixth," he said.

"Do you know what time of day?"

"Must have been pretty late. I remember her telling me that her dad had to wake up the midwives. But how come you're asking?"

"I'm trying to give her the stars," I said. "I'll explain later. Thanks, Justin."

I went and got the phone book, and you know what? They have a listing for astrologers in the yellow pages.

I looked at the ads and called the astrologer with the nicest-looking face. Her name was Allison Antares.

I told her about Ileana's book and about how stars were the one thing she liked best that I didn't have in the book yet. And I thought that if I had an astrology chart from the time she was born, that would be a way of giving them to her.

Allison Antares liked that so well she laughed and said she'd be delighted to help. She didn't even charge me.

"No interpretation, of course. I would have to charge for that. But I'll be happy to run up a natal chart as a gift. She must be a very lucky young woman to have such a sensitive boy in her life."

"Uh . . . right," I agreed, feeling my face get hot.

A couple of days later, the chart came in the mail. It was a beautiful wheel covered with those neat signs astrologers use. At the top it said *Natal Chart for Ileana Antonescu* in flowing script. I pasted it onto the last page of Ileana's book and was ready for the party.

SLIGHTLY HEROIC

Saturday finally came. Exactly at two o'clock, my dad dropped me off in front of the Antonescus' house. It was the first time I'd seen it. It was huge, sort of like the White House, but bigger. It had columns all across the front and a long sloping lawn, which was all dead grass and mud now. The walk that led up to it was wide enough for a truck.

There were jenti kids coming from every direction. The street was full of the fancy, old-fashioned cars dropping them off. Every one of the kids looked at me through their dark glasses like they wondered who had let the pig loose in the yard.

I hung around by the gates—Ileana's house had gates, of course—hoping Justin would show up so that we could go in together. The jenti went past me, gave me their escaped-pig look, and passed on in silence. I could hear music coming from inside the house. Violins, playing something classical.

Gregor arrived with his gang. When they saw me, he motioned for them to wait and came over to me.

"What are you doing here?" he growled. "You cannot be invited."

I didn't say anything. I just looked him up and down like I thought his mother had dressed him funny.

"Show me your invitation!" he demanded.

"Show me yours. Or are you here to help with the dishes?"

Gregor loomed over me. "Gadje, whatever Ileana may say, you do not belong here. If you go into that house, then whether you are marked or not, I will find a way to be revenged."

I held out my hand and studied my nails. "Look at that. Sheer terror," I said.

Gregor clenched his fist and shook it in my face. He really did. Then he spun around and went back to his friends. They marched past the gate to the house.

I stood there while the lines of jenti tapered off and the street emptied out. As far as I could tell, no other gadje had been invited. If they had been, they hadn't shown up. And still there was no sign of Justin.

The wind was cold. Finally it pushed me inside.

You know those movies where the crazy family in the old house has a nine-foot-tall butler who looks like Frankenstein's monster? The Antonescus' butler was only seven feet tall and looked like Dracula.

"Welcome, young sir. I am Ignatz. May I have your name?" He sort of purred, if tigers purr.

"Cody Elliot," I told him.

While we were talking, someone was taking my present from me and someone else was helping me off with my coat.

"Ah, Master Elliot. There are particular instructions concerning you. This is your first visit to the Antonescus', is it not? Szasz, convey Master Elliot to the ballroom."

Of course Ileana's house would have a ballroom. It was probably right over the indoor polo field.

Szasz, who did look like Frankenstein's monster, led me down a long hall and into a sort of courtyard—I know, houses don't have courtyards, but that's what this was—and up a sweeping staircase. I had never seen a sweeping staircase before, but there it was, like something in one of Mom and Dad's old movies. It rose in a long, graceful curve like it wanted to fly and stopped at the second floor. There were double doors standing open there, and the music I had heard was coming through them.

When I walked into the ballroom, all the jenti turned and looked at me. Then they turned their backs. I just stood there for a minute, not daring to go farther into the room and not knowing what I was supposed to do.

Then Ileana came sailing through the crowd toward me with her hand held out. She was wearing a beautiful white dress and one dark red rose over her heart.

"So you have come at last," she said. "I have been waiting for you."

"I was hanging around out front," I explained. "I kind of wanted to come in with Justin."

"He will not be able to come. He is ill," Ileana said, and her face fell. "It is good you came in."

"What's the matter?" I asked.

"He did not say," she said sadly. "Come, I must introduce you to some people." Then she took me by the arm and led me over to her parents. "Papa, you will remember Cody Elliot. Mama, this is the boy who helped Justin that day."

"It's very good to see you again," Mr. Antonescu said, shaking my hand. "I've heard fine things from Ileana about your writing."

Why did he have to bring that up?

Mrs. Antonescu smiled. She looked like Ileana, small and very beautiful.

"Ah, the young hero," she said in a strong jenti accent.

"And how are you finding Vlad Dracul?" Mr. Antonescu asked me.

"Oh, uh, different," I said. "Very different."

"Yes. I suppose it is." Mr. Antonescu smiled. "But I wonder if you are enjoying it there."

I could have said something polite, but Mr. Antonescu didn't seem like the kind of guy to be fooled by politeness.

"There's no law that says you have to enjoy school," I said. "I like Ileana and Justin and the natatorium when I'm alone in the pool. The rest you can keep."

Mr. Antonescu turned to Ileana. "A good, honest answer," he said. "Refreshing, especially in my profession, to hear one like it. Thank you."

I had the feeling I'd failed some kind of test.

"Come," said Ileana. "I will show you where you will be sitting."

There were long tables at one end of the room. I saw that they had little place cards by every plate.

At the far end of the room was one table turned at a right angle to all the others. It was set up on a dais, and there were chairs along only one side of it, so they faced everyone else in the room.

"This will be yours," Ileana said.

My seat was right by hers.

"Now I must introduce you to some of my other friends," Ileana said.

She took me over to a couple of girls.

"Marie and Erzabet, this is Cody Elliot," she said. "Cody, these are Marie and Erzabet Haraszthy. They are also at our table."

"How do you do," they purred.

"I must ask you to excuse me," Ileana said. "There are others to whom I must say hello."

The three of us stood there, smiling the way people do when they don't know what else to do. Actually, they were smiling down on me. Marie, the shorter one, was half a head taller than I was. Erzabet was bigger than that.

"So, do you go to Vlad?" I asked Erzabet's shoulder.

"Vlad?" she said carefully, like she wasn't used to speaking English. "No. No, we are not from the United States."

"We are true Transylvanians," Marie answered, smiling at me like I was the best-looking sandwich she'd ever seen.

"Though, to be sure, our families have lived in Paris for many years," Erzabet went on. "Because of the Communists in Hungary and Romania, it was necessary. Now we stay because—well, because it is Paris."

"Though we spend part of each year in—excuse me, *on*—the ancestral lands," Marie said. "It is necessary to feel connected to one's place, don't you agree?"

"Actually, yeah," I said. "I'm from California and I miss it a lot."

"A gadje from California," Erzabet said. "That is something I have never met before."

Marie put her hand on my arm.

"You must explain to us how you know our Ileana," she said.

I wasn't going to tell these girls about Illyria. They acted like they were fifteen going on thirty-seven. Sophisticated, I mean.

"We're classmates," I said. "Ileana and Justin—do you know Justin Warrener, by the way?—and I. We hang out together a lot."

"Ah. You hang out," Erzabet said, like I had said something funny and she was trying not to laugh.

"How pleasant it must be to hang out," Marie said. "We have no opportunity to do so at home."

"We must always be at doing something in Europe," Erzabet said. "It is expected."

"They keep us pretty busy at Vlad, too," I said.

"But still, you find time to hang out," Marie said.

"After school," I said.

Marie and Erzabet gave each other one of those mysterious grins that girls share. The ones that make boys feel like toads. Then they turned their beautiful, glowing eyes on me like I was a joke they didn't quite get.

"So, are you over here for long?" I asked, trying to fill up the silence.

"No. We are returning to Europe quite soon," Erzabet said. "We only came because of the importance of Ileana's birthday."

"You come over every year for her birthday?" I asked.

"Hardly," Marie said. "As you must know, the fifteenth year is most important among us."

"I hadn't heard," I said.

"You will have observed the rose she wears," Erzabet said. "It means she is a woman now."

"No more a little girl in any respect," Marie said.

"In Europe she would already know who her husband was going to be," Erzabet said. "But here . . ." She waved one hand like she was brushing something away.

"Here, even the jenti do not mature as they should," Marie said. "And that is a pity for her, given who she is—"

"But it is not for us to be critical," Erzabet interrupted.

"No, certainly not," Marie said.

"Things are different in America," Erzabet said. "In Europe we would never see a gadje at such a ceremony as this." And she smiled at me again.

It made me mad, that smile.

"Yeah," I said. "You know what America's like. We'll let anybody in. Even vampires. 'Scuse me." I smiled back and left.

Charming people at this party. Where was Justin when I needed him?

Dad had given me his cell phone so that I could call for a ride home when I needed it. I went out onto the landing and dialed Justin's number.

"Hello?" I recognized Mrs. Warrener's beautiful voice.

"Mrs. Warrener, it's Cody Elliot," I said. "I was just wondering how Justin is."

"Justin will be well in a day or two," she said, sounding sad. She paused. "It's only that our blood supply ran out a little early this month. I don't believe Justin ever told you, but he needs somewhat more than the average, and this month—he just had to use up what we had."

I heard her sob and stop herself.

"How are you feeling, Mrs. Warrener?" I asked.

"Oh, I'm quite well, thank you. I won't need to—to drink for a few days. By then, we'll have some money in the house again."

"Could I speak to Justin, please?" I said.

"One moment."

"Hello," Justin whispered.

"Hey, man. I'm at Ileana's party and everyone's looking at me like I'm on the menu," I said. "I don't even know anyone here but Ileana and Gregor and his gang. Help."

"I can't come, you know that," he said bitterly. "My mother explained why."

"But if you got some—some people juice, could you make it?" I asked.

Justin sighed. "It's the only place I want to be."

"Then why don't I just tell Ileana to send over a gallon? They must have vats of it here."

There was a long, long silence on the other end of the line.

Finally Justin said, "Can't do that. Can't ask."

"What is it, some kind of rule you guys have against sharing?"

"No," Justin said after a minute. "It's not a jenti thing. It's an old New England thing. It's a me thing. We . . . I . . . just can't ask her, that's all."

Inside my head, I said some really choice things about Justin and his damned pride. I almost said, "Okay, then," and hung up. Then I thought about sitting in that dining room full of Erzabets and Maries, and instead I said, "Get ready. I'm coming over."

"Stay at the party," Justin whispered. "Ileana wants you there."

"She wants you here," I said. "So I'm coming over to give you a drink. And you're not asking me, I'm telling you."

Man, I sounded brave. A lot braver than I felt.

"No! You're my friend. And Ileana's marked you." I heard the phone making weird little thumping sounds. Justin had dropped it.

"I'll ask her nicely," I said. "I want you sitting up and ready to party when I get there."

I couldn't believe I was doing this. My head was spinning with fear. But I needed him as much as he needed me.

I went back in and found Ileana.

"I know what's wrong with Justin," I said. "I can get him here, but I need your permission to do something."

"What?"

"You have to let me . . . give him a drink of your private stock," I said.

Ileana's golden eyes got big. Then she smiled like the sun coming up.

I must be in love. Even her canines look cute.

"You would do this for him? You would bring my friend to me?" she said, putting her hand on my arm.

"If you say I can. And if somebody can give me a lift," I said.

She said something to me in vampire, which I didn't understand a word of, but I liked the way she said it, a lot. Then she spoke to one of the servants.

He led me quickly through the house, down into the kitchens, and out into a heated garage the size of an airplane hangar. A chauffeur appeared out of nowhere and opened the door of a limo for me.

"You know where we're going?" I asked him.

"Indeed, sir," he said, and he clicked his heels together.

Anyway, we were at Justin's in twenty minutes.

"Can you wait?" I asked.

"Certainly, sir, as long as it takes. I am at your service."

I went up and knocked on the door. I was all set to say something funny to cover my nervousness, but when I saw Mrs. Warrener's face, I couldn't.

"He's waiting for you," she said.

Justin was sitting up in a chair with most of his tux on. The jacket was hanging on the door and his sleeve was rolled up. He tried to raise his head when I came in, but he couldn't.

There were tubes and needles on a little table beside him and a chair for me.

I took off my jacket, sat down, and rolled up my sleeve.

"I hope you know I like you," I said. "I hate needles."

"There's the good old-fashioned way if you'd rather," he gasped.

"Needle," I said.

Mrs. Warrener cleaned my arm with alcohol and stuck the needle in like she was giving me a kiss. She gave me a rubber thing to hold on to and said to keep the pressure in my fist constant.

I'm making it sound like a big deal, but it didn't feel like anything, really. Apart from the dizzy, scared part, which I was doing to myself.

But it was something to Justin. He gasped like a drowning man coming back to life. He threw back his head, and I saw his fangs. One leg trembled. Then, as my blood began to move through him, the fangs got shorter and shorter and the trembling in his leg stopped.

Actually, it was very ugly. No wonder the jenti have the reputation they do.

In a few minutes, Justin shook his head like he'd been knocked out and was coming back to consciousness. Then he smiled at me.

"That's the second time you've done the nicest thing for me anyone's ever done," he said.

"You can pay me back by going to that damn party with me," I said. "The limo's waiting."

Mrs. Warrener took away the needles and things and I rolled down my sleeve.

"You'd better rest a little, Cody," she said. "I think you may be a bit light-headed. Let me get you some chocolate cookies."

"I'm fine," I said, standing up and falling over backward with my feet in the air.

They put me on a couch, and Justin and Mrs. Warrener sat beside me. She was looking worried; he was smiling.

"Okay, I'll have those cookies," I said.

I sat up, and after about half a bag, I felt better.

"By the way," Justin said. "What did Ileana say when you told her you wanted to do this for me?"

"Something in jenti. Don't ask me what."

"I'll bet I know what she said." And he repeated it.

"Yeah, that was it," I said. "How did you know?"

"It's just something I picked up from her when we were kids," he said. "It's a blessing: 'Fly home straight and safe.' Come on, let's party."

HAPPY BIRTHDAY, PRINCESS

When we went back out to the car, the chauffeur opened the door, bowed, and clicked his heels again.

"Guy really gets into it," I said as we settled back into the seat.

"He should," Justin said. "You're somebody."

We walked back into the ballroom just before they started to serve dessert. There must have been more than two hundred people who lifted their heads and stared at us as we stood in the doorway. There had been the sounds of music and talking as we came up the stairs, but now the room was absolutely silent.

"Uh-oh, we're late," I whispered.

Mr. Antonescu got up from his place and came over to us.

"How are you boys?" he asked. "Are you all right, both of you?"

"I am now," Justin said.

"Sure," I said.

Mr. Antonescu guided us up to the head table. Ileana was seated in the center, with Gregor beside her and her mother next to him. The chairs on the other side of her were empty.

"Oh, goody, we get to eat with Gregor," I whispered.

"Oh, yeah, couldn't not seat him here," Justin said. "He's her cousin."

As we crossed the room, Ileana stood up. She said a few words in jenti, and everybody else stood up, too—even Gregor, who got up last of all, looking like a yard dog on a short chain. Mr. Antonescu pulled our chairs out for us. Still nobody in the room said a word.

Justin and I stood there with a whole room of jenti staring at us, and, from the looks on their faces, they didn't know any more about what was going on than I did.

Then Ileana whispered, "Be seated, sir," and I realized she meant me.

So I sat down, and she sat down, and the whole room sat down.

"Justin, you are quite well?" Ileana said across me.

Justin's answer was a grin, and a sign he made with two fingers. He crooked them like hooks and made a little grabbing motion downward.

Ileana put her napkin to her face and laughed silently into it. Her shoulders shook.

"What's so funny?" I demanded.

"Nothing," Justin said. "I just told her how okay I was."

"How okay are you?" I said. "What was that thing with the hand? Why did everybody stand up?"

"That thing with the hand is a gesture among us," Ileana said, gasping to keep from laughing. "It means now the same thing as saying 'okay.' But long ago it meant 'I have feasted.'"

"Cute," I said.

"And the reason everyone stood up is because they cannot remain seated in my presence on such a day. And the reason I stood up is to honor you, poet-knight of Illyria."

Under the table she took my hand and squeezed it.

"Oh. Well. Hey," I said. I could feel myself blushing.

She nodded to the musicians, and they started playing again. The desserts came in and were whisked down in front of us. When the covers came off the plates, I saw that Justin and I had two each. Nobody else did.

"Eat," Ileana said. "You must restore your sugars. It is little enough."

As usual with jenti food, I didn't know what I was eating, and I'd never tasted anything better.

While I was eating, Ileana whispered, "I heard about what you said to Erzabet and Marie. That was quite funny, though very rude. I will wager no one has called them vampires to their faces before in their lives."

Then Gregor said something to her, and she turned to answer him.

"Have you met Marie and Erzabet?" I asked Justin. "Geez."

"No, but I bet I know the kind you're talking about," Justin said. "Real Old Country, right?"

"We are true Transylvanians," I said, trying to copy their accent. "They made me feel like a bug."

Justin laughed.

"That kind don't think much of American jenti, either," he said. "Don't worry about them. I think they're really kind of jealous of what we have here."

"I can see why they would be," I said, looking around the ballroom. "This place must be worth a fortune."

"I didn't mean that," Justin said. "Most of these folks have plenty of money. I was thinking about the freedom."

"They've got freedom in Europe," I said.

"Not like we have it here," he said. "I'm talking about the freedom to be what you want. Do what you want with your life. Maybe you think the jenti in New Sodom haven't got much, compared to the gadje. Maybe we haven't. But compared to the old ways, we've come pretty far. And in Europe they've stayed behind."

"Marie was saying that in Europe Ileana would already know who her husband would be," I said.

"She'd know a lot more than that," Justin said. "But she'd be kind of a special case, even in Europe."

"Heck, she'd be a special case anywhere," I said.

"Yeah, but you know what I mean," Justin said.

I was just about to ask him what he did mean, but Ileana rang a small crystal bell sitting in front of her, and the whole room was filled with that delicate sound.

The music stopped and everyone looked at her.

She stood up.

"Forgive me, friends, if I speak in English rather than the ancestral speech," she said. "But there are some among us today who do not know our mother tongue, and I would not exclude them from what I have to say. And also, I am an American. This is the language I use most every day. And I love the beauty of English very much."

There was a little stir out there at the tables. It sounded like leather wings rustling.

Ileana went on. "I wish to thank you all for honoring me with your presence here today. Among us a girl's Fifteenth is one of the most important days of her life. To be able to share it with so many who mean so much to my family and me is a dear splendor."

She turned to her father, who was sitting at the head of the first table on her right.

"First, I wish to thank the father who loved my mother so much and came together with her to bring me life. And I thank the mother who brought me out of darkness and into light."

She bowed slightly to her mother, who smiled.

"I wish to thank all the uncles and aunts and cousins and friends from abroad who have connected me to the old ways and taught me their sweetness. But I wish to thank also the friends I have made who are different from us for teaching me the sweetness of the new."

I heard that rustle again. I didn't think they liked what they were hearing.

"We are a great people," Ileana said. "Nothing has ever defeated or destroyed us. We are strong as the stones in our Mother Earth. And because we are, we can afford to be less afraid. The world has changed and is changing. I believe we are being called to a new kind of greatness, a time when jenti and gadje will have no fear of each other."

I'm not sure, but I think Gregor growled at that point.

Ileana said just one more thing. "I believe that time has come."

She rang the little bell once more and sat down. The music started again.

Under his breath, so that only I could hear, Justin whistled the first few notes of "The Star-Spangled Banner" and added "Oh, boy," like he couldn't believe what he'd just heard.

"What?" I whispered.

"Later," he said.

"Now," I said, but as I said it the presents were brought in.

There were hundreds of them, piled up on carts the size of pickup trucks.

One by one, they were unwrapped by Szasz while Ignatz read out the cards that said who each gift was from.

They were the sort of presents any girl gets when she turns fifteen. Antique jewelry, sculptures, paintings, a couple of land grants, the deed to a diamond mine in South Africa, just the usual stuff.

As each gift was announced, the jenti applauded. They clapped in unison, starting slowly and working up to a speed so high they couldn't keep together anymore, when the rhythm dissolved into a wave of pleasure.

After each gift, Ileana said something to the giver.

All this took quite a while, and that gave me plenty of time to compare my gift with the others. I felt myself getting smaller and smaller inside. And more and more confused. How did Ileana rate so high with these people? What was I missing?

About halfway through the proceedings, Szasz unwrapped the gift from Cody Elliot. Ignatz held it up and announced, "The gift of Master Cody Elliot. A book, the title of which is . . ." He paused, flipped through the book, and said, "A blank book with . . . objects pasted onto some of the pages?"

Gregor laughed. A few other people tittered.

"Let me see it," Ileana commanded, and I mean she commanded.

Ignatz brought it up to her.

Ileana flipped through the pages carefully. "A page of clouds," she said. "A page of beautiful feathers from my favorite bird. Golden oak leaves. And here on the last page, the stars. My own stars. Yes. And the rest of the pages for me to fill in with the days of my life." She turned to me. "Thank you, friend. You are always so generous to me."

She put the book beside her and sat down.

Ileana's mother started the clapping, but this time only a few people joined in, and it died out almost as soon as it began. Szasz held up the next gift.

Finally, the whole hideous thing was over. The carts were wheeled away, the tables were carried out of the room, and the orchestra started again. Now they were playing wild Gypsy music, and the jenti, the perfect, controlled jenti, started dancing to it.

It was incredible. They threw themselves around the room like a pack of dogs fighting. I didn't even know people could bend like that, let alone do it in formal clothes. And they did it with perfect control. Nobody ever bumped into anybody else, or even missed a step.

And who danced with Ileana? Gregor. He lifted her and spun her like she was cotton candy. Ileana moved with him like she was part of his arm. And nobody tried to cut in on him.

I hated it.

"He's holding her pretty close for a cousin," I said to Justin at one point.

"There are cousins and cousins," Justin said.

"Meaning what exactly?"

"A lot of people expect them to get married," Justin said.

"What? But they're related."

"A lot of people marry people they're related to," Justin said. "I'll bet you didn't know that more than half of all the presidents have been related to at least one other president."

"Gregor is not going to be president," I snapped.

"No, but Ileana's going to be kind of a queen someday," Justin said.

"Oh, give me a break."

Justin looked at me funny. "You don't know, do you? She never told you." He shook his head. "She should have. I wonder why she didn't."

"What are you talking about?"

"The jenti sort of have their own royalty," Justin said.

"Ileana's pretty high up. Her mother is queen of the jenti in a lot of Europe. Here, too."

"This is America, she's an American," I said in my best Patrick Henry style. "We left that stuff behind a long time ago."

"Yep. But some of it follows some of us around," Justin said. "I don't think Ileana likes it much. But there's not a whole lot she can do about it."

"So she's got to marry Gregor just because some people think she's a queen? How does he rate?" I said, getting madder and madder.

"He's pretty high up, too."

"What's he? The king?"

"The jenti don't have kings, just queens," Justin said. "But he's high enough to marry her."

"This stinks. I'm getting out of here,"

"It's bad manners to leave before her mother does," Justin said.

"Who cares? I'm just a dumb gadje. Nobody wants me here anyway."

Justin put his hand on my sleeve. "She does. Don't leave without letting her know you're going."

I shook him off.

"I'm out of here," I said.

But Justin put his hand back and clamped down with all the strength of the vampire he was. "Look, don't run away without giving her a chance to say good-bye to you. You don't understand everything that's going on here."

"I understand enough," I said.

"No, I don't think so," Justin said. "You're probably the first gadje who's ever been invited to a Fifteenth.

You're definitely the first one who was ever invited to sit at the head table. And you're right, nobody else wants you here. Not her parents, not any of her relatives. And you can pretty well guess what Gregor thinks about it. Do you get what I'm saying?"

"No, and let go of me, damn it."

"Why would she do that?"

I didn't say anything.

"Now, wait here for a minute," Justin said. "Please, Cody. I don't want to have to break your legs."

So I sat there and fumed while Justin disappeared into the dancers. I waited a long time—it seemed like a long time—and finally I got tired of it. If Justin was going to break my legs, he was going to have to hunt me down first.

Just then, I felt a hand on my shoulder.

"Please to come with me, sir," Ignatz said.

"I'm leaving," I said.

"I have no wish to detain you, sir, but your hosts have requested you particularly. Please to follow."

There's something about being asked nicely by a seven-foot-tall vampire that makes anything seem like a good idea, so I went down the hall with him into a little room filled with shadows and dim, warm light. Mr. Antonescu was there with his wife and Ileana.

As I went in, Mrs. Antonescu curtsied to me. Mr. Antonescu bowed.

"We understand you wish to leave," Mr. Antonescu said. "Please forgive us, Cody, that we did not thank you properly as soon as you came back with Justin. It seemed best not to interrupt Ileana's Fifteenth to do so. Perhaps we were wrong. It is not always easy to know the proper thing to do, even with a lifetime of practice."

"It's not that," I said. "I—I just need to get home, that's all. I wouldn't have wanted you to interrupt Ileana's party."

"I wish now to do something improper," Mrs. Antonescu said. And she kissed me on the cheek. "You are great of heart and generous."

"There are legends among the jenti about gadje like you," Mr. Antonescu said. "But I've never met one before."

"All I did was give a little blood."

"Yes. You gave it. You gave it without bargaining, or even being asked," Mrs. Antonescu said. "That is everything."

"You are in some danger of becoming a hero among us," Mr. Antonescu said.

"No," I said. "I mean, please don't tell anybody. It was no big deal."

"Mother and Father, may I speak to my friend alone for a moment?" Ileana asked.

Her parents looked at each other.

"Briefly, darling. You have guests," Mr. Antonescu said.

"Yes, Papa," she said.

Ileana stood there in the half light, looking like the queen she was. I couldn't think of a thing to say.

Finally, she said something. "Thank you."

"You're welcome."

"You know Justin is my oldest friend. You brought him here to me. It was noble of you."

"Nobility is just another free service we offer."

"Please," she said. "I know you are witty, but do not be witty just now. There is something I must tell you."

"If it's about Gregor, I already know."

"You do not know this. Even Justin does not know it. No one knows it but I. I will not marry Gregor, ever. If I ever marry anyone, it will be someone I wish to marry. Only someone I love."

"Oh. Well. Good," I said.

She looked at me like she was waiting for me to say something else.

"Good night," she said finally. "I must return to my party."

She walked past me, and as she did, she brushed my cheek with her lips.

I turned to her and tried to hold her, but I sort of lost my balance and ended up kissing the air when I was aiming for her face.

"My poet," she whispered.

Then she slipped away, and I heard the door click shut.

The big limo was as quiet as a graveyard at midnight. It had been waiting for me. Ignatz had seen me to the front door and even held an umbrella over my head while I got in. It had started to rain, and the windows were covered with coatings of silver. The chauffeur's head on the other side of the glass was the only other human thing in the world now. I mean, it was private.

Which gave me a lot of time to tell myself what a jerk I'd been. Couldn't even kiss a girl who wanted me to kiss her. But I'd been thrown off balance in more ways than one. I still was. The most I'd hoped for was that maybe sometime soon Ileana would go to the movies with me. Now I'd found out she was some kind of a queen-in-training and was thinking about getting married. Hello, we're fifteen here! Let me finish my junior year first, at least.

Plus, there was that damn poet thing again.

And I loved Ileana, but how much? And did she love me? Or was I misreading her friendship and her gratitude for my helping Justin?

It felt like life had gotten suddenly serious. I had myself pretty well tied in knots by the time I got home.

Mom and Dad were watching another of their ancient movies when I went in.

"How was it, dear?" Mom said, reaching for the remote and freezing the image.

"All right," I said.

"Who gave you a lift home?" Dad asked.

"Ileana's chauffeur," I said.

"Ho, ho, *ho*," said Dad. "Were you being honored, or did they just want to get rid of you early?"

"They wanted to get rid of me early," I said. "I threw up in the punch bowl after we played spin the bottle."

"I just asked," Dad said.

"You made a joke," I said. "I made one back."

"Touché, Jack," Mom said.

"So may we take it that you did have a good time?" Dad asked.

"Memorable," I said. "It was memorable."

"Memorable is good," Mom said.

The picture on the screen was of some guy kissing the

girl he was in love with. He looked like he'd never missed a pair of lips in his life. He had it easy. All he had to do was look ahead to the last page of the script to see how it came out.

"You can start up your movie again. I'm going to bed," I said.

MR. HORVATH QUOTES A POEM

When the limo came for me Monday morning, the chauffeur saluted and insisted on carrying my books. The other kids inside moved over for me. One made a double mocha on the espresso machine and offered it to me. And not one word of jenti did they speak until we got to school.

As soon as I hit the campus, I could feel that something was different. Up and down the halls, jenti nodded as they passed me. A few real outspoken ones even said "Good morning." From jenti, that was like being slapped on the back.

When I got to math class, Mr. Mach came over to my desk and said, "You know, Elliot, your work shows progress. I'm thinking of grading your papers in light of that. What do you think?"

"I think it's about time."

Mr. Mach nodded. "You're right, it is."

When I went into English, Shadwell caught me at the door.

"Ah, Elliot, how's the epic coming?"

I shook my head.

"Writer's block?" he asked.

"No, I'm just a lousy writer," I admitted.

"Well, let me know if I can help," he said. "God knows, the epic isn't the only form of literature. You may have other talents that you're not aware of. Of course, time is short. But if there's anything I can do." He gave me a little bow.

In social studies, Mr. Gibbon took me aside.

"I have noted considerable progress in your work, Elliot," he said. "But your grasp of the subtleties of this discipline leaves something to be desired."

"I'm sorry, Mr. Gibbon," I said. "I like social studies, but I just can't keep straight all the names of the people who were involved in the Second Defenestration of Prague in 1619."

"It was 1618, actually," Mr. Gibbon said. "But I should dislike to give you a less-than-passing grade. Perhaps we might consider a paper on some special topic of particular interest to you, which you might present to me. It would be factored into your overall grade."

"You mean a real research paper? For a real grade?"

"Exactly, Elliot," he said.

"You're on," I said. "But what kind of thing do you have in mind?"

"Oh, perhaps something pertaining to the history of the jenti in America," he said, looking at the ceiling. "Quite a few of us have made an impact, you know. Benedict Arnold. Aaron Burr. Jefferson Davis. A number of others. I suggest you consult Whittaker's *The Silent Heritage*, which is the standard work on the subject, and bring me your proposal by the end of the week."

Ms. Vukovitch spoke to me after class.

"So what are you doing free period on Mondays and Wednesdays?"

"Nothing special," I said.

"I want you to spend them with me. Just us. I'm gonna tutor you till you think like Leonardo, or Einstein, or maybe even like me. Okay?"

"Yes, ma'am," I said.

"Looking forward to it, gadje boy," she said, and she gave me a smile that felt like a kiss.

So I had what I wanted. They were going to grade me like a jenti. And I was going to have to work harder than ever. I couldn't believe how good it felt.

I suppose I should have been expecting to get called into Horvath's office.

"Master Cody," he said, looking at me over the points of his long fingers. "Master Cody." He paused like he couldn't think of what to say next. His tongue flicked in and out. "It seems you are the hero of the hour."

"I don't know what you mean, sir," I said.

"Such modesty. And from a gadje." I guessed he'd forgotten the day when he'd told me that term was never used here.

He got up and walked over to the fire. When he

turned back to me, his face was in shadow. I think he wanted that.

"You have done a noble thing, Master Cody," he said, sounding like he hated the words. "But our ways are not your ways. And there are complications you know nothing of. No one can blame you for not knowing what you have not been told. So I will tell you now, and I expect you to act on the knowledge in the future. Community relations in New Sodom are delicate. It is the responsibility of all of us, jenti and gadje alike, to keep them in balance so that everyone may benefit. We need each other. But we cannot become each other, nor should we wish to do so." He paused. "But I see I am not persuading you."

"That's probably because I don't know what you're talking about," I said.

"Ah," he said. "Thank you. I will be more direct. I want no more gadje heroics. I want no more . . . fraternization between you and your jenti classmates. No more breaking down of wholesome barriers. It endangers the delicate relations I spoke of. Do you understand that?"

"So you want me to be like Blatt and Barzini and Falbo?"

"Young men whose families have been in our community for generations. They understand the way things work, and how beneficial it is that they do so. I would advise you to be guided by them," Horvath said.

"Here's what I don't get," I said. "What I think you're talking about didn't happen at school. So where do you get off telling me what to do with my own time?"

"I occupy a high enough place in this community to see it whole," Horvath said. "I am aware, as you are not, of how intricate are the webs that bind things together. I don't wish to discount what you did for Master Warrener. In itself, it was a noble act. But it is sending out vibrations along the complex filaments that bind us together as a people and connect us as a community to our neighbors. Moreover, your attendance at Miss Antonescu's party was extremely ill advised."

"Just a minute," I said, jumping out of my chair like Dad raising an objection in court. "Who do you think you are, telling me where I can and can't go? I was invited, for pete's sake."

"You misunderstand," Horvath said smoothly. "Sit down. It is certainly not my place to tell the Antonescus whom they may and may not have in their home—"

"Damn straight," I said.

"Mind your tongue. We are not in your gadje locker room now, boy," Horvath snapped. "And I already told you to sit down."

I sat. Then I crossed my legs and made a little temple with my fingers the way Horvath liked to do.

"It is not my place to tell the Antonescus whom they may entertain," he went on. "But frankly, your presence in their home on Saturday gave great offense to others, others nearly as important as they."

" 'Others' meaning Gregor Dimitru, right?"

Horvath went on like he hadn't heard me, so I knew I was right.

"The Antonescus' invitation, while a generous act, was a lapse in judgment," he said, "and had you been raised here, you would have known better than to accept. Let me give you some words from one of our fine

157

old New England poets. You have heard of Robert Frost, I hope?"

I nodded.

"In 'Mending Wall' he tells us, 'Good fences make good neighbors,'" Horvath said.

I knew that poem. It was in Shadwell's textbook.

"Isn't that the one that also says, 'Something there is that doesn't love a wall'?" I asked.

Horvath glared at me.

"Mr. Horvath," I said, trying to keep my voice from trembling with anger and fear, "when I came here you told me that some things at this school might seem strange to me at first. You said I could come to you for explanations. Well, as you keep saying, I'm not from around here. It seems like I have some ways that are strange to you, and I'd better explain them. First of all, I make friends with people I like. Second, I don't like to be told what to do by you when I'm not on this campus. Third, you ain't seen nothing yet. Does that help?"

"Leave my office," Horvath growled.

I did.

WORDS AND SILENCES

After that, I didn't need anybody to tell me that Horvath had it in for me. But Justin did anyway.

We were at the natatorium. It was late afternoon. Ever since Ileana's Fifteenth, Justin had been meeting me there on the days when we didn't go to his place to study. He'd come in about the time the rest of the gadjes split and watch me splash around for a while, like he was trying to figure out how I did it. It was funny; he hated water as much as any jenti, but it seemed to fascinate him, too. I hadn't noticed that with any of the others.

Today he was actually sitting hunched up on the diving board.

When I saw him, I put my head down and swam over to him underwater, coming up slowly so I didn't splash him.

"Hey, man," I said. "You'd better get off that thing. Diving boards can be hazardous to jenti health."

"Just wanted to see what it felt like being surrounded by water," he said.

"How does it feel?" I asked him.

"Kind of dry doing it this way," he said. He smiled; then he stopped. "Did you hear that Horvath's trying to find a gadje kid to replace you?"

"No," I said. "Who told you?"

"There's a kid I know who volunteers in his office after school," Justin said. "She heard him making phone calls all over town trying to find some gadje willing to come here so that he can expel you."

"Expel me? For what?" I said.

"He's the principal. He can make something up," Justin said. "Anyway, this girl wanted me to let you know."

"Thanks for telling me," I snapped, kicking over to the side of the pool so hard I nearly splashed him. "Damn Horvath. He finally gets a gadje who wants to go here and he tries to get rid of him."

"He's mad at the teachers, too," Justin added. "He wants them to stop giving you real grades, but they won't back down. What I mean is, don't worry too much. He can't get rid of you unless he has a kid to replace you, and that won't be easy. The old families are afraid to send their kids to Vlad. And they look down on anybody who does. Most of the gadje we get are kids who've flunked out of everywhere else."

I put my head back on the edge of the pool and rolled it from side to side. I didn't need this, too. Even with all the help I was getting from Justin, Ileana, and Ms. Vukovitch, I was swimming in oatmeal. It wasn't that I wasn't learning; I was learning plenty. But the more I learned, the less I knew. I was getting D+ in math, D in social studies, C in gym, like everybody else. D in science, A in water polo. No one got a grade in English until the end of the year, but I knew what mine was going to be. All I had to turn in was my lousy half-finished epic.

But my biggest worry was Ileana. Everybody had been different to me since I'd let Justin tank up on the day of her Fifteenth, but nobody had been more different than she was. On the surface, things were the same. Homework, Illyria. Dinner together at school. Sometimes we followed the ancient gadje ritual of hanging out. But the silence that had come down between us was still there. It wasn't an empty silence. There was something she was waiting for me to say. I knew that, and I thought I knew what it was. I just didn't know if I was ready to say it.

I felt like a sailor, coming to the coast of Illyria for the first time and at night, wondering what would happen if I set foot on shore.

On Friday, when we went down into Justin's basement, Ileana sat with her arms wrapped around her legs while he put in a new harbor for Three Hills and I built a library next to the city hall in Palmyra.

"Ms. Shadwell can run it," I said. "We'll put in a wing for the collected works of Anaxander and Vasco, right next to the one for *Dracula*. Of course, it'll be a pretty big wing. Your poets will have to write some more books to fill it."

Ileana said, "They cannot sing their old songs any-more. And they are waiting to hear their new ones."

"Oh," I said.

"Ah," she sighed.

Over the weekend, Mom and Dad had an unusual idea: They decided to go out to see a movie.

"If you think you can tear yourself away from your academic pursuits for about two hours, we'd like you to accompany us," Dad said.

I was trying not to think about last Friday, and study-ing wasn't working, so I said, "Sure."

We went downtown.

"This isn't the way to the multiplex," I said. "It's back toward the interstate."

"In the old days before civilization had attained the heights represented by twenty-screen nickelodeons with Styrofoam walls, theaters were located in urban areas and had only one screen," Dad said. "It is to such a place that we go now."

"The Loring Theatre is what's called an art house," Mom explained. "It shows films you can't see anywhere else."

"We've been meaning to go for months," Dad said. "But I've been too damned busy. I'm still too busy, in fact. But your mother and I are not going to miss this film."

"What is it?"

"*Beauty and the Beast,*" Dad said.

"What's the big deal?" I said. "We saw that when I was a little kid."

"The *real Beauty and the Beast,*" Dad said.

"By Jean Cocteau," Mom said. "One of the classics of French cinema."

When we got to the Loring Theatre, I could tell it was a jenti place. It had that old-fashioned respectable look they like, and all the cars around it were the jenti kind. Ancient, dark, and special.

When Dad went up to the ticket window, the girl behind it looked at him like someone had just deposited dead fish in front of her. Then she saw me.

"One moment, sir," she said, and disappeared into the back.

A minute later, a jenti in a tuxedo came out. "Master Elliot and family, I am Mr. Chernak," he said. "I have the honor to be the manager of this establishment. Please to come in."

"We have to get our tickets," Dad said.

"This is your first visit, I believe?" asked Mr. Chernak. "Please accept the hospitality of our theater." And he threw one arm out toward the doors.

We followed him in. He led us to seats on the aisle and said, "What refreshments may I offer you? We have all the usual beverages and sweets, as well as a full coffee bar."

"Nothing, thanks," Dad said, looking confused.

Mr. Chernak looked like he'd been stabbed. "Nothing?" he gasped. "Sir, our double café au lait is the perfect complement to this film. I urge you to try it."

"Yes, please," Mom said. She was anxious not to hurt his feelings. "May we have three?"

Mr. Chernak disappeared and came back with three tall, white-topped coffee drinks, just as the curtain—this place had a curtain—went up.

"Welcome," he said. "Please to enjoy your stay."

"Why do I feel like I've just been knighted by Vlad Dracul?" Dad said. "And how did he know our name?"

"Shhh," said Mom.

So we saw the real *Beauty and the Beast*. It's a very good movie, and I recommend it. But not when you're trying not to think about love.

● ● ●

Monday started out to be very ordinary. Until I saw Ileana, at least. By now, she was all I could think about. In fact, I was thinking about her so much that I could hardly talk to her. And she was listening hard for what she wanted me to say.

Dinner, where she and Justin and I shared the table with Brian Blatt, was kind of a relief. We never said anything until he finished feeding and left, but that never took him long. When he got up to go, it was the first time I was ever sorry to see him leave. But I still didn't say anything, and neither did Ileana.

Justin did. "It's warmer today."

Then a shadow fell across the table and we all looked up. It was Gregor. He gave Ileana a little bow and spoke to her in jenti.

She answered him with one word. Then she said, "You may speak English here, Gregor. Everyone else at this table does."

"What I have to say is not for everyone's ears," he said.

"Then it is not for mine, either," Ileana told him.

"May I sit down, princess?" he asked.

"You may, if you conduct yourself properly," Ileana told him.

Gregor yanked back the empty chair and plunked himself into it. He sighed like a steam engine and put his fists on the table. Then he turned to Justin.

"I wish to apologize," he said. "For the business of the creek."

Justin looked at his food.

"I know I'm supposed to say 'That's okay,'" he said finally. "But I can't. It's not. Trying to throw one of us in the water. It's close to murder."

"There was not so much water there," Gregor said.

"That's true," Justin allowed. "But I hadn't done anything to you."

"If you had, I would not be offering the apology," Gregor said. "But I had some reason to think you had done something to me. So my act is not without explanation, even if I was wrong."

"Okay, what's the explanation?" Justin said.

"As I said before I sat down, what I have to say is not for everyone to hear."

Gregor looked funny. He looked like he was blushing.

Suddenly, I knew what he was trying to say. He'd thought Justin and Ileana might have a thing for each other, and that had made him do it.

"Anything you have say to me, you can say in front of my friends," Justin said. "Otherwise, I don't want to hear it."

"You do not accept my apology, then?" Gregor asked.

"Can't," Justin said. "Sorry."

Gregor stood up. He was furious.

"Then I withdraw it," he said. And he added something in vampire. Whatever it was, it made Ileana turn white.

Gregor left.

"What'd he say?" I asked.

"Just something stupid," Justin said.

"It was not something stupid, it was something vile," Ileana told me. "A kind of threat. And an insult. He told Justin, 'May your last fang rot in your head.' Among us that is as bad as an insult gets."

"You don't need to tell him the rest," Justin said.

"I think I must," Ileana said. "He implied that you and Justin are lovers."

I felt myself getting hot with anger. Justin was bent over like Gregor had punched him in the stomach.

Well, Justin had stuck up for me with Brian Blatt, and I was going to do the same for him. I stood up.

"Hey, Gregor," I shouted. "I hear your mama's so fat she sells shade."

Gregor turned around. It got real quiet in the dining hall.

"Yeah," I went on. "I hear your mother is so fat, when she went shopping, she put on a pair of BVDs, and by the time she got home, they spelled BOULE-VARD."

He took a step toward me. Then he stopped. Behind him, some kids laughed.

"Hey, Gregor, you know what?" I added. "Your mama is so fat, when she ran away from home, they had to use all four sides of the milk carton."

Practically the whole room laughed at that one.

Gregor spun around. Then most of the rest of the room laughed.

When he turned back to me, I could tell I had gotten him. There were tears starting in his eyes. He raised his fists. His pale face turned bright red. He pulled back his lips and I could see that his fangs were out. But he didn't come toward me. He just stood there, trembling with rage while the laughter died.

"That's just what I heard." I shrugged.

Gregor stamped out of the dining hall. One last ripple of laughter followed him out.

Justin was rocking from side to side, laughing into his hands.

But Ileana was furious. She sat staring at her plate, her hand clamped on her fork. Her face was as red as Gregor's.

"What did you do that for?" she snapped.

"Because of what he said about Justin and me, of course."

"What you did was much worse."

"It was not."

"Yes, it was. You insulted his mother, not him," she said. "And you only dared to do it because you know you are marked and he cannot touch you."

"That's a lie," I said, and it was. I'd been so mad I'd forgotten all about that marked gadje stuff for a minute. "I can't believe you're sticking up for him."

"I am not sticking up, as you put it, for anyone," Ileana said. "But you were completely wrong to do what you did."

"Check this out," I said. "No one's wrong to stick up for a friend."

"That may be what you call it, but that is not what it was," she said. "No jenti would have said what you said. You should be ashamed. As ashamed as I am to be sitting with you."

"Ashamed?" I shouted. "Well, guess what, princess. I'm not a jenti. Remember?"

That made the whole room turn and look at us.

"No," Ileana said quietly. "You are not a jenti. And you are not what I thought you were. You are a liar and a disgusting gadje pig, and I do not want to sit with you anymore."

She got up from the table and moved all the way across the room and sat down with some girls.

I stared after her, feeling the jenti eyes on us both. Something in the room was changing. Going back to the way it had been.

"What the hell is wrong with her?" I muttered finally.

Justin shook his head. "Ileana's got a lot of dignity," he said. "You hurt it, doing that while she was here."

"Well, what was I supposed to do? Just sit there and let him insult you?"

"I appreciate what you did," Justin said. "But I'm not Ileana."

"What did she mean, I'm not who she thought I was?"

"What she said, I guess," Justin replied. "You figure it out."

"Well, I'm just a dumb gadje," I said. "I'm not fit to hang out with princesses anyway."

I got up from the table.

"I'll see you in science," Justin said.

I didn't answer.

• • •

I didn't go to science. What was the point? Ms. Vukovitch might as well have been teaching it in jenti-speak as far as I was concerned. And if Justin took an hour to explain it to me after school, so what? I still didn't really get it. How could I, when I didn't have the years of background every jenti kid had?

But that wasn't really what was bothering me. I already knew I wasn't good enough for this school. I wasn't good enough for Ileana. Ileana the beautiful and brilliant and royal, who always did everything right, because she knew all the rules in this place, and I never would.

I thought of my "epic" again and cringed. My English class at Cotton Mather had been on page twelve of *Macbeth*. That was about my speed. Maybe I should go back and see if they'd made it to the end of act 1 yet. But what would that solve? Nothing. I didn't belong there, either.

I went down to the creek. It was even smaller now than it had been when Gregor and his gang had tried to throw Justin into it. A miserable little trickle ran through the dirty snow, under a sky just as dirty. The water moved fast, without going anywhere. It looked lost.

I took a look around at the beautiful buildings with their lights glowing dimly behind the dark-tinted glass, where the elegant, quiet, smart strangers were busy learning the things that made them better than me. And Ileana was their damn princess.

No matter how hard I tried, I'd never be good enough.

It was a long way home. I started to walk.

BRAMS

Mom was surprised when I came home early, and on foot, but she believed me when I told her I wasn't feeling well.

"With this filthy winter weather, I'm surprised we're not all sick all the time," she said.

"I'm not exactly sick," I said. "I pulled a muscle in gym. I'll be okay in a day or two. I guess."

And I limped upstairs, went into my room, and sat in the dark.

Justin called that night.

"Didn't see you in class this afternoon," he said. "Wondered if everything was all right."

"No," I said.

There was a pause. Then Justin said, "Anything I can do to help?"

"No," I said.

"See you tomorrow?"

"No," I said. "Not tomorrow."

"Oh. Okay. See you Wednesday, then," Justin said.

"I don't know," I said. "I don't know when I'm coming back." *Or if.*

"Well," he said, and he paused again, "want to come over Friday after school and do Illyria?"

"No," I said. "Not this week."

Justin sighed. "Okay," he said. "See you."

"See you."

There is a place you can go that is below down and beyond bad. When you get there, every minute that passes goes by like an hour. Every hour that passes feels like an achievement without a goal. And everything around you makes you hurt. I was in that place now, my own personal anti-Illyria. And there was no one I could even tell about it. I just sat in my room, wrapped in my shame and pain.

I stayed in my room. When Dad asked me what was wrong, I told him "Nothing." When Mom wanted to take me to the doctor, I said no. They let me alone after that. I think they knew that what was wrong wasn't anything a doctor could help. Nothing could.

Justin called six times. Three times the first day, twice the second day, and once the third. My mom took the calls.

Ileana never called.

On Friday, Dad said, "Cody, either you go to school today or I'm taking you to the hospital."

"It'd be a waste of time," I said.

"Which one, the school or the hospital?" Dad said.

"Either one," I said. "Can't we go home?"

He came into my room and sat down on my bed.

"No, Cody, much as I'd like to, I don't think we can," he said.

I raised my head. "You mean you want to go back to California?"

"It's home to me, too," he sighed. "Every morning when I get up and look out the window and see that filthy snow in the yard, I feel like killing myself."

"Well, then, why don't we?" I asked.

"Because it's my career," Dad said. "In California, I'd reached a dead end. You know I wasn't happy at Billings, Billings and Billings, but you don't know everything about why. It wasn't just that they wouldn't promote me. It was that they were telling other firms I wasn't as good as I looked. They were lying about me to keep anyone else from hiring me away."

I couldn't believe grown-ups would do something like that. Then I thought of Horvath.

"So I wrote to a few friends here in Massachusetts," he said. "You know I went to law school in this state. I was able to use their help to get me admitted to the Massachusetts bar on motion. I imagine you know what that is?"

"Without having to take the bar exam," I said.

Dad nodded. "A professional courtesy. And Leach, Swindol and Twist took me like that." He snapped his fingers. "Now I have a chance at last to be the kind of lawyer I always saw myself as when I was grinding out those three years in law school. And, not incidentally, a chance to give your mother and you a much higher quality of life than we've ever had before."

"What quality of life are you talking about?" I said. "You're not happy, I'm not happy, and I'm sure Mom isn't happy."

"I'm talking about things like this house," Dad said. "You like it, don't you?"

"It's okay," I said. "But every time you go outside, you're still in Massachusetts."

"I know you don't like it here," Dad said. "But remember this. You don't have to stay forever. When you finish high school, in not much more than three years, you'll have the option of going to college somewhere back home. I'm assuming your grades from Vlad will be as good as everyone else's.

"As for your mother and me, we have each other, and I have my work, which, believe it or not, I find very satisfying. In a few years, if I score some really good cases, we may be returning ourselves. Perhaps we'll even be able to retire early. It's amazing how much business they get at Leach, Swindol and Twist."

For the first time, I was seeing how different my father and I were. I could never care enough about a life full of stuff to make myself and my whole family miserable to get it. And I was pretty sure that if I had a kid like me, I'd want to find out what was wrong with him rather than explaining myself, the way he just had. But Dad, I decided, was Dad. He was who he was and he couldn't be anyone else. Not with me, at least. It was too bad, but it was just one more thing.

"Now, if there's something wrong at school, maybe I can help," Dad said. "Is there something you'd like me to speak to Horvath about?"

"Nope," I said, standing up. "I guess I'll get ready to go."

So my body went to school on Friday. It sat in the classes, and I think it maybe even took notes. It ate at dinner and it ran around in gym. It ignored Ileana and it spoke a couple of times to Justin. But I wasn't there. I don't know where I was.

Finally, I went to the natatorium. I was alone in there, but so what? I was alone everywhere. I didn't give a thought to where the other Impalers were.

As I came out of the locker room, my feet went out from under me, and the next thing I knew, Barzini was kicking me. He had his shoes on.

As I tried to get up, I noticed Louis Lapierre and Brian Blatt holding a piece of clear plastic fishing line at ankle height. They were, of course, laughing.

"Guess what, stoker?" Barzini said. "Horvath found another gadje. My brother. He starts Monday."

He kicked me in the ribs.

"So now, who needs you?"

He kicked me again as I tried to get up. Blatt and Lapierre grabbed my arms.

"Thought we'd forget about this, didn't you, stoker?" Barzini said.

Kick.

"Told you you were gonna die."

"You think too much," Blatt said, and laughed some more.

"Go, Barzini!" said Lapierre.

Barzini kicked me again. I gasped. I was sure the next kick would break my ribs. But there was no next kick.

Instead, there was the sound of Barzini howling and Justin's voice saying something like, "Know something? That's not nice."

Then Barzini was sort of flying over my head on his way to the pool, and there was a loud splash in the middle of it.

Then Brian Blatt followed him, making a sound that might have been "Help" but sounded more like *"Hooooooolph."*

Lapierre did some begging and cursing as Justin picked him up and heaved him overhead. Then there was another splash, and the three of them were in the middle of the pool, calling us names.

And Justin was standing at the pool's edge with his arms folded. Vampire strength. Justin had just as much of it as any jenti when he wanted to use it. That thin little arm had held me in place with no trouble at all at Ileana's Fifteenth.

I tried to get up. Barzini had done a worse number on me than Gregor or Ilie, but I seemed to be basically all right—if intense physical pain and an inability to raise yourself from the floor qualify as basically all right.

Barzini paddled to the opposite side of the pool and started to climb out.

"Nope," Justin said. "Not till we say you can."

Barzini cursed him.

"You don't really want to make me mad, do you?" Justin said.

Actually, I think he was mad already. His fangs were out.

Lapierre started to whine.

"Come on, let us out," he said. "These are our school clothes."

Justin just shook his head.

"Want me to let them out?" he whispered to me.

"Yeah, okay," I said. The look in Justin's eyes was even more frightening than his fangs.

"Okay, we're going to let you go," Justin said. "But if you ever gang up on Cody again, you're all a bunch of brams. Brams. Do you know what that means?"

I could tell from the looks on their faces that Blatt and Barzini and Lapierre knew exactly what it meant. They scrambled up out of the pool and ran to the lockers.

Justin turned to me and whispered, "I've always wanted to say something like that."

"Thanks," I said. "If you hadn't come along, they'd have stomped me flat."

Justin nodded. "You all right?" he asked.

"I've felt better," I said. "But nothing's broken."

"Let's sit down for a minute," Justin said. "Give those brams a chance to leave."

He helped me limp over to a bench.

"How'd you happen to show up just then?" I asked. "You're supposed to be in the library."

"Oh. I heard something like this might happen," he said. "Those guys talk pretty loud."

I felt my throat get tight.

"Know something?" I said when I was sure I could talk. "You're the best friend I ever had."

"You too," Justin said.

We heard the outer doors of the natatorium slam. The gray light from the windows high behind the bleachers faded, and the water in the pool turned dark.

Finally I said, "Would it be okay if you helped me get home? Maybe you could stay for dinner."

"Sure," my best friend said.

MR. HORVATH TALKS
TO CHARON

Justin helped me limp to a limo and went home with me.

Mom had a fit when we came through the door. She called Dad to come home, and when he saw how I looked, he was ready to sue the school, the township, the families of the rest of the team, and the Commonwealth of Massachusetts. But Justin and I got them calmed down after a while.

When they were cooled off, Mom and Dad adopted Justin and gave him a car—okay, not really, but that was their attitude. I told them the truth—that he'd saved me from getting beaten up much worse than I had been. I didn't mention anything about how a little guy like him could do that, and they didn't ask. It was enough that he'd saved precious me. Justin glowed under their praise.

I guess he hadn't had much of that in his life. When Dad drove us back to his house that night, he introduced himself to Mrs. Warrener and told her all the things he'd already told Justin. By then, my friend was so happy he was almost crying. Even as banged up as I was, seeing him so happy made me feel better.

That was the good part. That, and getting to lie around for a couple of days being waited on hand and foot.

· · ·

The bad stuff came Monday when I went back to Vlad. Mom and Dad both wanted me to stay home, but I wasn't going to give my buddies on the team that satisfaction.

It turned out I didn't need to worry about that.

Just before nine o'clock, Ms. Prentiss came into math class and asked me to report to Mr. Horvath.

Justin was already there. He was sitting on the big sofa, hunched over. Charon was in his usual place under the table. He looked up when I came in.

"Master Cody. Sit down," Horvath said. He didn't sound happy.

I sat down next to Justin. Horvath started pacing in front of us.

"Do you boys know what you have done to this school?" he asked finally.

What we've done to the school? Yeah. Exactly nothing. What is this about?

"You have caused the loss of three of our best water polo players," Horvath said. "As well as the loss of a new member of the team," he almost shouted. "I have had calls this morning—most unpleasant calls, I might add—from the families of Master Blatt, Master Barzini, and Master Lapierre. All of them are withdrawing from this school because of the vicious and unprovoked attack you two made on them Friday afternoon."

"Wait a minute," I said. "They jumped me. All Justin did was—"

"Be silent," Horvath snapped. "Because of your actions, Vlad Dracul now has too few players to participate in the next round of water polo matches, only a few days from now. This will place us on probation with the state and may cause us to lose our accreditation if the missed games cannot be made up. The future existence of this school may be at stake. Do you boys know how hard it is to get gadje to come here?" He growled something in jenti that I was glad I couldn't understand. Then, in a calmer voice, he went on. "If it were possible to persuade the families of our departing students to remain by offering them your expulsions, you would already be gone."

Justin gasped.

"Unfortunately, that is not an option they are prepared to accept," Horvath went on. "They are afraid that some other jent—some other student might attack them in the same unprovoked way that Master Justin did Friday." He turned to Justin. "Such a naked display of aggression is something I never would have expected from you, of all people. You have been raised to know how fragile is the tolerance that makes New Sodom the refuge it is for—for all of us. Such an act may have repercussions far beyond the walls of this place."

"I'm sorry, sir." Justin bowed his head.

"Sorry. Yes, I should think you would be, Master Justin," Horvath said. "One should expect nothing more from Master Cody than that he should act as what he is. But you. You have known all your life what was expected of you."

"I do know what's expected of me, sir," Justin said.

"Then you agree that there is no excuse for what you did. Good. Because while I still need this gadje, I have no particular need of you. Quite the contrary, in fact. And I have decided to expel you. You will never be allowed to return to Vlad Dracul."

Justin went white.

"Just a minute," I said. "Those three guys jumped me. Barzini tried to beat me to a pulp while the other two held me down. Are you saying Justin should have let them do it?"

"That is enough!" Horvath shouted at me. He leveled his finger at my nose. He had very long fingers, and the nails were filed to points. "You will—"

But I never found out what I would do because at that moment, Charon raised his head. That was all he did, raise his head and look at Horvath. But Horvath stopped talking. I mean, he stopped talking to me. He started having this one-sided conversation with Charon.

"You do not understand," he said to the wolf. "It is not as simple as they wish to make it."

There was silence. But it felt like something was going on in that silence.

"I am not being dishonorable. I am protecting the school," Horvath said.

Silence. Charon's big yellow eyes just kept looking at Horvath.

"No. I will not," Horvath said.

More silence and more eyes.

"I will not do it."

Something in Charon's face changed. It didn't look like a threat, any more than Charon's expressions always looked like threats. It reminded me of the way Charon had looked at me the first time he saw me. Sort of bored and contemptuous.

Horvath saw it, too.

"Very well," he said. And he turned back to me and Justin. "It may be that you have some right on your side after all," he said. "In any case, no purpose will be served by punishing you. The damage is done. You may go."

Charon's tail hit the floor like the rap of a gavel.

Horvath stood up. He took a deep breath and closed his eyes. "It may be that I have spoken somewhat too hastily, in my anxiety for the school. If so . . ." He gulped. "I apologize."

Charon's head went back down on the floor. He closed one eye.

Justin went out ahead of me, holding himself as straight as a ruler, keeping control.

Charon's one open eye met mine. I did the most jenti thing I could think of. I bowed.

The big yellow eye closed, then opened.

I wouldn't swear it was a wink, but on the other hand, it couldn't have been anything else.

DIVING IN

If you think Tracy, Falbo, and Pyrek missed Barzini and Blatt and Lapierre, you're wrong. None of the Impalers liked each other, it turned out. In fact, they were glad they were gone.

"Barzini and them were the biggest creeps on the team, Elliot," Tracy told me that afternoon. "Next to you, anyway."

"Hey, Elliot, get Tracy thrown out, too," Falbo said. "He sucks."

Tracy replied that it was Falbo who sucked, and they debated that while I got my trunks on.

Underskinker came out of his office and gave me a dirty look.

"I don't allow no fightin' on my team," he said.

"Neither does Justin Warrener," I said.

"Who?"

"He's the guy who stopped the fight. The fight on your team," I said. "You should meet him sometime."

"I don't need to meet no more damn vampires," Underskinker said.

"They prefer to be called jenti," I said. "Vampire's kind of an insult. Makes 'em mad. You want to be more careful, Coach."

"No fightin' on duh team!" Underskinker roared.

I went out to the pool, with Underskinker trundling along behind.

"Okay, you punks, here it is," he said. "We gadda find three more guys to be on dis team and we gadda do it in a week. I wancha to go out and find 'em. Udderwise . . ." He paused. I think he was trying to imagine a life without his swivel chair and his case of beer. "Udderwise, sumtin' bad's gonna happen."

He left us to work that one out and headed back to his office.

"Geez, why do we have to do it?" Falbo complained.

"Because they can't," I said. "Horvath tried. Maybe even Underskinker tried. But who do they really know? You guys have lived here all your lives, right? Don't you have any friends? Maybe a brother like Barzini did?"

"I ain't got no brother," Falbo said.

"His parents took one look at him and stopped trying," Tracy said. "But Pyrek's got two brothers."

"One's five, one's twenty," Pyrek said.

"How about a sister, then?" I said. "I never read a rule that says water polo can't be coed."

Tracy gave me a disgusted look. "Barzini musta kicked you in the head, not the ribs," he said.

"Well, our next game, if we show up for it, is a week from today," I said. "If we can't come up with some players, we may all end up back at Cotton Mather."

"Homework," Falbo whispered.

"Real grades." Tracy shook his head.

"It's all your fault, Elliot, you fix it," Pyrek pleaded.

"Well," Tracy said. "If we only got a few days more of the sweet life, I'm going to enjoy 'em."

He headed for the locker room, followed by Falbo and Pyrek.

I eased myself into the water and tried to swim. It still hurt, and my chest had more colors than a rainfall map of Brazil, but I thought it would be good for me to move around. I was right. In a few minutes, I was loosening up a little.

I wasn't alone for long, though. Justin came in as soon as the Impalers left.

I swam over to him.

"How are you feeling?" Justin asked.

"Not bad, for how bad I feel," I said. "How about you?"

"Still scared, I guess," Justin said.

"Yeah, well, I guess we've all got something to worry about with this water polo thing," I said. "You think they'll really close the school?"

"It's complicated." Justin sighed. "The gadje in New Sodom want to keep this place because it keeps us out of their school. But they hate paying for it. I can't say that I blame them, either. Their own kids don't have anything half as nice. But a lot of our money comes from the state. And the state doesn't care whether there's a school for jenti or not. There are some people on the state board who'd like to see us shut down."

"Why does everything have to be so complicated?"

"Things just are, that's all."

"I don't suppose you have any gadje friends."

"Just you."

"Water polo," I said, getting out of the pool to sit beside him. "Close down a whole school over water polo."

"It'd be about more than that," Justin said. "Water polo would just be the excuse."

I noticed I was dripping onto Justin's leg. I jerked away.

"Oh, geez, Justin, I'm sorry," I said.

"Oh, it's just a little," he said, wiping it with his sleeve. He looked out at the warm green water, where the last of my ripples were fading away.

"I'd sure love to do what you do. Just once. Just to know what my fish feel like."

"Why don't you?" I said.

"Are you crazy, or do you just think I am?" Justin demanded.

"Neither one," I said. "But you've never been in water, right?"

"Of course not."

"Then how do you really know what would happen to you?" I asked.

"Because it happens to all of us," he said. "Always has. I told you."

"Justin, have you ever known another jenti who wanted anything to do with swimming?"

"Not really."

"Did you ever know another jenti who raised fish?"

"There's a girl in social studies named Helen Danforth. She has a bowl of guppies," Justin said.

"I'm not trying to talk you into anything," I said. "But, Justin, you're so different from the rest of the jenti in some ways, maybe you're different in this way, too."

Justin didn't answer. He just looked at the water and bit his lip. Finally he said, "How deep is the shallow end, three feet?"

I nodded.

"If I got in, I could get out again real fast if I had to," he said. "You'd be right there, right?"

"Of course I would."

"Let's get me a suit," he said.

We found him a suit and a bag. I picked up about forty extra towels, just in case. I hoped I didn't look as scared as I felt.

I got in first.

"Okay," I said, faking a smile. "Nothing to it. Just take it one step at a time."

Justin had set his face like there was a brick wall in front of him and he was working out how he was going to put his head through it. He faced the pool and took one step down the ladder. The water washed over his foot. He stopped.

"How does that feel?" I asked.

"Not bad," he decided after a minute.

He brought his other foot down to join it.

"Pretty good," he said.

He came down another step and stood up to his thighs in water.

"How are you feeling?" I asked. I was ready to drag him out by his hair.

"Funny," he said. "Real funny."

That was it. I reached to lock my arm around his neck and pull him out, but before I could, Justin had thrown himself flat. With a splash, he disappeared under the water and shot away from me.

"Justin!" I called. "Justin, don't! Wait a minute! Wait for me! Just wait!"

But Justin couldn't have heard me anyway.

I saw an arrow of water curving away from the place where his head was, streaking across the pool, faster than anybody I'd ever seen. Then, down by the diving board, he came up.

"Yippee!"

You've never heard anybody actually shout "Yippee!" in your life, right? Well, neither had I. But Justin did. And then he leapt out of the water. And as he soared five, ten feet into the air, I saw he wasn't Justin anymore.

Where my friend had been was a dark, streamlined creature covered with sleek brown fur. It looked human, but the way a human would look if it was redesigned for living in water.

It reached the top of its leap, curved over gracefully, splashed down, and shot over to me.

"This is so great," Justin said. "I wish I'd done this years ago. Come on."

But there was no way I could keep up with him. He rocketed back and forth through the water, curving in long sweeps, zigzagging, jumping, and diving. It was like he was taking possession of the pool.

I just stayed in the middle calling things like, "Justin, maybe you shouldn't . . . ," "Maybe you need to . . . ," and "It's only your first time."

But he was born for what he was doing.

Finally, he popped up beside me, smiled, and said, "This is the third time you've saved me."

"What?"

"First you saved me from Gregor, then you saved me from missing Ileana's party. Now you've saved me from never finding out who I really am," he said.

"You know, it's getting late," I said. "We'd better dry off."

"I don't ever want to be dry again."

"Come on. The custodians will be coming around to close the pool and wake up Underskinker."

"Okay," Justin said reluctantly. He glided over to the edge of the pool and popped out of the water.

As he toweled himself off, he turned back into the Justin I knew. But there was a difference. He was smiling, and there was no shyness in it. He was happy, and he knew no one could take that happiness away from him. He even walked differently.

We got our clothes on and went out into the early dark. The snow had retreated into corners and shady places now. It glowed faintly.

"So anyway," Justin said, like he had been thinking it over, "what do I have to do to get on the water polo team? For real, I mean."

The idea was so simple it was brilliant. And I was sure Horvath would hate it. But then I had my own idea, which was either as brilliant as Justin's or bone stupid. I knew how to get Justin on the team and how to save the school's accreditation. And how to keep Horvath from interfering.

There was just one possible hitch.

"I've already got that figured out," I said. "But that won't be good enough. We need two or three more players. Justin—do you think there are any more jenti around who can do what you do?"

"There might be," Justin said after a few minutes. "That girl I mentioned, Helen, the one with the guppies. And her brother Carlton. They say he got into a wading pool when he was three. Scared the daylights out of his mom."

"That'd be three," I said.

"I can think of a few more who might," Justin said. "The funny thing is, they're all like me. Kind of small and brown-haired. Or blondish. And they've all got that problem I've got, needing extra blood sometimes. And none of them transforms. But every one of them does something with water, even if it's only running the sprinkler."

"Okay," I said, trying to think of everything at once. "The important thing is to keep Horvath from finding out. That means we have to have tryouts at some other place. Do you know anybody who's got their own pool?"

"Actually, yes," Justin said. "There's a boy named Thornton Ames I could ask. His family have had a pool for years, just for looks. They never use it, of course. But they keep it up and everything. You know, to fit in."

"Could we use it this Saturday, with no grown-ups around?" I asked.

"It'll be complicated," Justin said. "But we'll see."

TRYOUTS

Sometimes everything just falls into place. It turned out that Thornton Ames's parents were going into Boston for a matinee that Saturday, so we had their pool to use. And Thornton was interested. So were Helen and Carlton Danforth.

We all met at the Ames place at two o'clock.

It was a bright, windy day, with the steam blowing off the water in streamers. Justin and I were shivering in our suits as the other three looked at us like we were a door they hadn't known was there and weren't sure they wanted to go through.

Just as Justin had said, they all were his physical type. They were so small and ordinary-looking that even when the three of them stood together, it looked like

there were two. I wondered if that ordinariness was another kind of vampire protection, for the ones who
couldn't fly away or become wolves at will.

"Okay," Justin said. "You all know what this is about.
Cody showed me how to change into something that
swims. It's the greatest feeling I've ever felt, and I guess
you are all interested, too, or you wouldn't be here. Just
to let you know, Cody and I will be right here to help you
out in case—well, in case it turns out this isn't your cup
of tea."

There was a big pile of towels nearby that Justin and
I had brought from Vlad. Helen Danforth looked gravely
at them. She looked at the water. Then she walked to the
edge of the pool, bent over, and dipped her finger into it.

"Nice and warm," she said thoughtfully.

"Let's see you do it, Justin," said Carlton.

Justin walked to the far end of the pool and jumped
in. Almost as soon as the water closed over his head, he
was changing into whatever it was he became.

I heard Helen gasp.

"Oh," Carlton breathed.

"Okay," Justin said, coming up. "Now Cody's going to
get in with me, and we're going to help any of you who
want to try."

The three of them just looked at us. Who could blame
them?

Finally, Helen said, "Well, I paid a lot of money for
this bathing suit thing. I might as well try it out."

She went into the house and came out again a few
minutes later in a one-piece suit that covered her almost
to her knees.

"Nobody dare laugh," she said.

"You look good," I said. "Very professional. Ready to try it?"

"Might as well," Helen said. "It's too cold out here."

She walked steadily down the steps of the pool until the water was up to her waist.

"Don't feel any different," she said.

"Maybe you need to put your head under," Justin said.

"I'll get down so only my head is sticking out," Helen replied, and she did.

"I still don't feel any different," she said. And then, "Oh, my!"

She stood up. From her neck down, she was sleek and web-footed and covered with brown fur.

She screamed and ducked her head under the water. When she came back up, her face was brown, furry, and smiling.

"This feels very nice," she said, and took off in the same kind of explosion of joy that Justin had the first time.

"Sister, be careful," Carlton said.

"Oh, pooh, get in yourself," she called to him.

"I think *I* will," Thornton said. He took off his clothes. His trunks were under them.

"Do I need to do anything else?" he asked.

"No, just get in," Justin said.

"I believe I'll jump," Carlton said, and he did.

"Carlton, you're supposed to take off your clothes first," Justin said when Carlton came back up, looking sort of like a seal in pants and a shirt.

"I'll remember next time," Carlton said. "I'm afraid I'm a little excited."

"Everyone look out, please," Thornton said, and threw himself into the water.

And there I was, one gadje with four jenti-otter-seal things all splashing around me like it was the most fun they'd ever had in their lives. I imagine it was.

It was nearly an hour before they calmed down.

"What do you suppose these things are that we've turned into?" Thornton asked, breathing hard. "It seems to me we ought to have a name."

"Never heard of anything like this happening to jenti before," Justin said.

"I think it must be some new ability that's grown up in us," Carlton said. "Maybe it's been in us for generations, waiting for Cody to find it. People can change."

"I've been giving it some thought," Helen said. "The British Isles have legends about creatures that can take the form of seals or people. They're called selkies. All of us here have ancestors that came from there. Maybe we're a sort of special British thing."

"Selkie. That's a good word," I said.

"It's as good as any," Justin said. "Let's be selkies."

"Let's swim some more," Thornton said, and they took off again, racing like otters around the pool.

It was nearly another hour before they calmed down enough for me to ask them, "Did Justin mention anything about water polo?"

"Of course," Helen said.

"We understand we're to be part of the team," Carlton said.

"I must say, it seems like it's going to be fun," Thornton said.

"I'll bet everyone's going to be surprised," Helen said.

"Everyone had better be surprised," I said. "Especially Horvath."

"We certainly won't tell him," Thornton said. "We'll all just volunteer to be replacements."

"But why wouldn't Mr. Horvath be glad to know that we can do this for the school?" Carlton asked.

"I don't actually know that he wouldn't," I said. "I don't know what to expect from him. But I know he doesn't like anything to change. So we have to present him and the state with something that they can't ignore or cover up."

"Just in case he'd rather let the school close than upset the old way of doing things," Justin said.

"Well, did anyone bring the rules for this game?" Helen asked.

We got out of the water and stood around shivering and looking at the two pages of rules that water polo has.

"Seems pretty clear," Thornton said.

"No problems that I can see," Carlton agreed.

"No indeed," said Helen. "I believe we're ready."

"Well, great," I said. I was anxious to get back in that warm water. "Somebody get a ball and we'll practice a little."

"What for?" Thornton said. "We know how to play. Besides, I'm afraid I don't own a ball. I think we ought to swim some more."

"But—" I began, then stopped. What difference did

it make if we practiced or not? The Impalers had never practiced before.

One after the other, the jenti leapt gracefully into the water and started doing things no gadje could ever do. I had a feeling that we were going to do quite a bit better in our next game than we'd ever done before.

Justin told me later that Horvath was surprised when all four of them went in at the same time to volunteer to be backups.

"This is highly irregular," he said. "We normally assign water polo as a duty."

"Yes, well, we want to do what we can to help out, sir," Justin had told him. "Especially me. After what I did last week."

Horvath gave him a hard look, but he assigned everyone lockers and ordered a special girl's suit in team colors for Helen.

This is just how it happened, and this was my part in it. There is one major thing I have left out. I have not put it in so far because there is no way to work it into the events I am describing. It was just there.

Ileana.

More accurately, the absence of Ileana.

My heart gnawed at me every minute, no matter what else I was doing, or seemed to be doing. In math class, where we sat beside each other, I never even looked at her. But not looking at her was all I could think about. And in the other classes, the ones I didn't have with her, I kept looking around for her.

Sometimes I smelled her when she was nowhere around. That was the worst and the weirdest.

But there is nothing more I can tell you about it than that. It just went on, the missing her, no matter what else I was doing.

Which probably explains somehow what happened with Gregor.

It was Wednesday. And it was beautiful. The air was soft as a kitten's breath, and the light was incredible. The little creek that ran through the campus was singing, and tiny little frogs called spring peepers were out and singing back to it.

I went down that way during free period, hoping to see one of those little frogs, but instead I saw Gregor. He was standing on the bank under a tree, looking at the water but not seeing it. He wasn't seeing the light, or the new green on the trees, or the flowers pushing open their petals. He looked like I felt. That was what did it.

I sort of went up behind him and said, "I'm sorry, Gregor. What I said was stupid, and I'm really sorry."

He didn't turn around, or answer me for a long time. Then he said, "It does not matter. You are a gadje. Nothing you say can hurt me."

I almost walked away. If I'd been feeling better, I would have. But I wasn't, so I said, "Even so, it was wrong. And I'm sorry I tried to hurt you."

He still didn't turn around. All he said was, "I hate this place. I hate you."

"That's funny," I said. "I hate it, too. I guess I hate you. I'm not sure."

"These filthy long winters. These endless summers that never cool off at night. Only Americans would live here by choice."

"I'm an American, and I wouldn't."

"Europe is beautiful, especially France," Gregor said.

"California," I said. "Especially the country south of San Francisco. And the redwoods on the coast. And San Diego. Even Los Angeles can look good when the wind blows the smog out to sea."

"It is nothing compared to the mountains of Norway, or the quiet of a single village street in Languedoc at twilight," Gregor said.

"Have you ever seen California?" I asked.

"I do not need to see it," Gregor said. "I have seen true beauty."

"I guess we're both a long way from home."

Gregor was silent again. Well, I'd tried to apologize.

"I'm going . . . ," I began.

"Thank you," Gregor said.

"But there's something else. Just in case it matters—whatever Ileana and I were, we're not anymore."

Gregor snickered. Then he said, "I suppose you are not a bad person, gadje. But you are abysmally stupid."

"Thanks," I said. "I like you, too."

I started back the way I'd come.

"We can be too proud," Gregor said. "All of us."

Whatever that meant.

But I was glad I'd done it.

Horvath was twisting in the wind. He got the game postponed another week and tried recruiting out of state, which is, I think, illegal, but this is Horvath we're talking about. Anyway, it didn't work.

There were rumors all week long that there wouldn't be a game, that the school would be put on probation.

That it might have to close. I heard the rumors being whispered in the dining hall. One kid even asked Mr. Shadwell if they'd be allowed to finish out the academic year. Shadwell said something about excellent standards, hundred-year history, worldwide reputation, not to worry. But he looked as scared as the kids.

Carlton and Justin and Helen and Thornton acted like they weren't sitting on the secret that was going to save the place. I really had to admire them. Knowing how fast word gets around among jenti, it was amazing that I never heard a thing about what was going to happen on the day of the next game.

And finally, the day came.

STATE STANDARDS

The day of the game, Horvath still didn't have a single new gadje for his team. If we couldn't even put enough guys in the water to start, we'd have to forfeit. A couple of dudes from the state's board of education had come out from Boston hoping to see us go down.

We saw them going up and down the halls all day, looking at everything, looking at us. Horvath was with them, and so was Charon. They wore suits, and they carried briefcases. Even so, they looked like jocks. They walked with the same rolling lurch that Under-skinker did, and their ties were strangling their thick necks. Big and tough as they were, though, they acted as scared as I'd felt my first day. They kept looking back over their shoulders like they were expecting to be

202

jumped. And Horvath looked like he was going to be hanged.

I almost wanted to go over and say to them, "Don't worry. Nobody's putting this school on suspension, or closing it. Enjoy the game." But, of course, I didn't.

During free period, I went down to the natatorium and got ready. Then I peeked into Underskinker's office. He wasn't there.

Tracy and Pyrek drifted in, and Falbo a few minutes later, looking sad.

"No more," Pyrek said sadly, and touched his locker like he was saying good-bye.

"Homework next week for sure," Tracy said.

"It's still your fault, Elliot," Falbo said. "Why didn't you do something, like I told you?"

"I did," I said.

"What? What'd you do?" Pyrek said, spinning around.

"You better be telling the truth," Tracy said, cocking his fist at me.

"It'll all be clear in a few minutes," I said. "Let's just say this: If the Impalers don't put a full team in the water to start, it'll be because you clowns don't get in."

"What do you mean?" Tracy said. "We always start out in the water. We just don't stay there."

"Anybody seen Underskinker?" I asked, to change the subject.

"Nope," Tracy and Pyrek said.

"We ought to see if we can find him," I said. "We've got a game and all."

Then we heard a huge crash from the back of the locker room.

When we got back there, Underskinker was lying on the floor with his head propped up against a locker and his feet splayed out. Three empty cases of Old Aroostook were beside him, and he had been working on the fourth.

"What's he doing back here?" Falbo said.

"Hiding," I said. I knelt down beside him. "Hey, Coach, we've got a game. Coach? Wake up. We've got a team, Coach. Come on, get out there and lead us the way you always do."

But Underskinker was gone.

"Oh, man," I said. "Look, we've got to get him on his feet. If those state guys see him like this, it won't be good. Can you guys bring him around? I've got to go back and meet our new teammates."

Pyrek and Tracy shrugged and started to shake Underskinker between them. Falbo stood at his feet and shouted, "Coach! Get up, Coach. Coach!" over and over again.

When I got back to the pool, the other team was arriving. It was our old friends from St. Biddulph's. They filed in quietly and took over some lockers. No one even looked at me.

Their coach came over to me.

"Where's Underskinker?" he asked.

"He's with the rest of the team," I said. "I expect him in a few minutes. Is there anything I can do for you, sir?"

"Yeah. You can tell him Coach Ryan says he's been waiting twenty years to see what's going to happen to him today. I hear you creeps can't even pretend to field a team now. He's gonna get his butt fired, and this whole damn school'll get closed down. And about time."

I cocked my head. "Maybe you'd rather tell him your-self, sir. After the game."

"Are you listening, creep?" Coach Ryan said. "There won't be a game."

"Are you forfeiting, sir?" I asked. "Because I don't know where you heard that we don't have a first string, but we do. And we're going to be ready to play when the whistle blows. Excuse me, sir. My teammates are com-ing."

The two "replacements" Horvath had drafted were coming grimly into the natatorium. Behind them came Justin, Helen, Carlton, and Thornton.

"Excuse me, where is the ladies' dressing room?" Helen asked me.

I took her over to the opposite side of the pool and left her. I wondered if this was the first time that locker room had ever been used.

"You bloodsuckers can't even swim," Ryan shouted. "Where's Underskinker?"

Falbo, Tracy, and Pyrek came out of the locker room shaking their heads.

"He's out," Pyrek said.

"We even threw water on him," Tracy added.

"So where are these guys you said are going to play on our team?" Falbo demanded.

Justin came out, with Carlton and Thornton behind him, and sat down on the bench.

"They'll be here when the whistle blows," I said, grinning.

The St. Biddulph's team came out and lined up at the far end of the pool. Coach Ryan went over to the half-distance line. A referee was already standing there.

"Where's Coach Underskinker?" he asked. "It's time to toss for sides." He had a quarter in his hand.

"I'm here for the coach," I said.

"I'm not tossing with a kid," Ryan said. "Anyway, where's your team?"

"If tossing's a problem for you, we'll just take the deep end," I said. "It doesn't matter to us."

"Does that satisfy you, Coach Ryan?" the referee asked.

"Sure," Ryan said. "Only there won't be a game."

I walked back to the deep end of the pool and took a quick look around. Falbo, Pyrek, and Tracy were standing in one corner. The jenti were sitting on their bench. Horvath, Charon, and the two suits had come in and climbed up to the bleachers. Judges and timekeepers were ready. And here came Helen in her new team bathing suit.

"I feel quite exposed," she said. "Let's get into the water quickly."

I looked over to Justin and gave him a thumbs-up. He replied with the two fingers that meant "I have feasted."

The whistle blew, and the St. Biddulph's Saints got into the shallow end and took position.

"Okay, let's get inna wadduh!" I shouted.

Pyrek, Tracy, Falbo, and I slid into the deep end. Justin and Carlton stood up and joined Helen.

"Let me make the introductions," I said. "Gadjes, jenti. Jenti, gadjes. Okay, Impalers, let's play ball."

Helen, Justin, and Carlton hit the water together, leaping out over the heads of the rest of the team.

I saw Horvath stand up and shout "No!" Charon was

on his feet, howling. But when my three friends raised their heads from the water, the howling stopped. In fact, it was dead quiet in the natatorium.

I looked up again at the bleachers. Charon, Horvath, and the two suits were all standing up with their hands (or paws) on the railing. Even the wolf looked surprised.

Three slim, graceful, dark-furred water creatures were hovering at the half-distance line.

"What's goin' on?" Ryan bellowed.

Then the referee blew his whistle again and tossed out the ball.

Justin raised his arm and slapped it straight into the St. Biddulph's goal.

The flags went up and waved for the point.

Back came the ball, and Helen sent it into the goal again.

It was ours now, and I took it, fired it at Carlton, and watched it sail into the goal a third time.

"Who are you guys?" Tracy shouted.

"Oh, we go here, same as you," Justin said.

"I had you in English a couple of years ago," Helen said to Tracy. "Though I don't suppose you'd remember. As I recall, you rarely came to class."

"Oh, yeah," Pyrek said. "I saw you in social studies one year."

"I thought you guys couldn't swim," Tracy said.

"Some can, some can't," Justin said, shrugging. "What do you say we finish this half now?"

Falbo said, "I'm not swimming with vamps. I'm getting out of here."

As soon as he did, Thornton slid in.

It really wasn't much of a game (but then our games never were). But it was a different kind of not much than we'd ever had before. The four jenti put the ball into the St. Biddulph's goal almost every time they hit it. When St. Biddulph's guys did manage to send it back to us, one of the jenti always intercepted it and sent it back at rocket speed. There wasn't anything for the gadje to do but play back and stay out of the way.

I decided to cover our goal, just in case. When I turned around to swim back to it, I noticed that our backup bench had disappeared. The fake replacements we had were gone. That seemed strange. They'd always stuck it out before.

Then, in a few minutes, they came back. They were in their street clothes and leading groups of friends into the bleachers.

The jenti came into the natatorium the way they did everything else—quietly. Even the sound of their feet on the steps was hushed. And nobody talked. They just watched us.

Every time I looked up, there were more of them. First they filled the seats on one side, then on the other. Word was spreading all over the campus. Even little jenti started to come in from the elementary school. The high school kids took them on their laps. By the end of the first half, it looked like the whole school was there.

Justin looked up at the packed, silent seats.

"Makes me kind of nervous," he said. "What if we don't do so well?"

"The score is two hundred and eleven to nothing," I said.

"Is that good?" he asked.

"We couldn't lose now if we stopped playing," I said.

"Frankly, I thought it would be more difficult," Thornton said. "Is this really all there is to it?"

"Well, yes," I said.

"I wonder why the state sets so much importance on it," Thornton said.

"Something about being well rounded, I imagine," Helen offered.

"That must be it," Carlton agreed.

Meanwhile, Ryan was raging up and down the natatorium.

"Underskinker. Where is Underskinker? I want Underskinker right now!"

And then our coach appeared. He came out of the locker room and braced himself in the doorway.

Ryan ran over to him, waving his finger in his face.

"You got no right to use vampires on your team," he shouted. "Human beings only. It says so in the rules. And if it don't, it should. I'm canceling this game."

I went over to them.

"Does that mean you're conceding?" I asked. "By the way, jenti are humans."

"We're not conceding, punk," Ryan raged. "We're just not playing. You get that, punk?"

"Hey!" Underskinker said. "Don't call dis punk a punk. Only I call my punks punks." Then he bent his head to me. "What's duh score?"

"Two hundred and eleven to nothing," I said. "It's the end of the first half."

Underskinker looked puzzled.

"Ryan, why you wanna quit with a lead like that?"

Ryan made a disgusted sound.

"Coach, it's our lead," I explained. "We're winning the game."

"Huh? How did dat happen?" Underskinker asked.

"I'll tell you later," I said.

"Okay," Underskinker agreed.

"I beg your pardon," Carlton, said coming over. "But we're beginning to dry off. Perhaps we ought to get back in the water."

"Nothing doing! We're out of here." Ryan stalked down toward his team, blowing his whistle and waving his arms. "C'mon, we're leaving!" he bellowed. "Move!"

"Do you concede, Coach?" one of the suits called down from the bleachers.

"You got to concede if you're leaving, Coach," the other suit said.

"Yeah!" Coach Ryan snapped, tearing off his baseball cap and throwing it into the pool.

As he stalked off with his team behind him, the jenti started to stand up. From somewhere high in the back of the bleachers the clapping started. It wasn't American-style clapping. It was European, everyone starting off slowly, keeping time, building up faster and faster until it exploded at the end, and it felt like the whole place was shaking.

There in the front row near Horvath was Gregor. He looked grim as always, but he was pounding away. So were his friends. So was Horvath.

"Hey, this is all right," said Pyrek.

"I could get used to this," said Tracy.

Justin, Helen, Carlton, and Thornton all lined up at the far end of the pool and bowed. As they did, the jenti cheered.

While they were doing that, Justin came over and got me. He walked me back with the others and raised my arm over my head.

Then the chant started, and it was Gregor who started it.

"Gad-*je*, gad-*je*, gad-*je*, gad-*je*."

The whole crowd was doing it.

The jenti swarmed over Justin, Carlton, Helen, and Thornton. It was like the dance at Ileana's party. All their cool was gone, and they flowed down from the bleachers like panthers. In a minute, each one of the selkies was the center of a circle of tall, dark, excited admirers.

I heard Helen saying, "It was all Justin's doing, you see. And Cody Elliot taught Justin. He taught all of us, really."

"He's our leader," I heard Thornton say.

"I believe the term is *captain*," Carlton said. "Though I'm not sure. I've never been on a team before."

Then more jenti crowded in between us and I couldn't hear anything else they said.

Horvath and Charon and the suits came down from the bleachers. Horvath was all over Underskinker, shaking his hand, slapping him on the back, congratulating him.

"Come on," I said to Justin. "We've got to hear what happens next."

"As you can see, gentlemen," Horvath was saying to the suits, "Vlad Dracul's water polo team is up to strength, and I daresay up to par. I trust your report to the state will reflect these realities."

"I don't know about that," the first suit said. "There were some irregularities here."

"Yeah," said the second suit. "Like, what are those things on your team?"

"Children, gentlemen. Students at Vlad Dracul. Am I right, son?" said my dad's voice behind me.

I turned around. Where had he come from?

"Son, are these your fellow students or not?" Dad asked again.

"Uh . . . yes," I said.

"Then what 'irregularities' can you possibly be referring to, gentlemen?" Dad said.

"You got to be a human being to play," said the second suit.

"Gentlemen, the law has yet to come to a final definition of what is and is not a human being," Dad said. "On the other hand, the civil rights laws are very precise on the matter of discrimination, and on the penalties for it. Permit me to introduce myself; I am Jack Elliot, a local attorney. I am here to tell you now that if there is any difficulty made by the state board on account of the way Vlad Dracul Magnet School chooses the particpants in its water sports, I will represent the school *pro bono publico*—that means at my own expense, in case you're not familiar with the term—in a class-action suit on behalf of these students. I can confidently predict that we will eventually win, and that the settlement we receive will bankrupt Massachusetts for the next hundred years. Now, we don't want that, do we?"

"Big-shot lawyer," said the first suit. "We got our own attorney."

"Did I neglect to mention that I am an associate at Leach, Swindol and Twist?" Dad said. "Perhaps you've heard of us?"

"Uh-oh," said the second suit.

Charon eyed them.

"Great game," said the first suit.

"Never saw anything like it, Coach," the second suit said.

They were still looking nervously at Charon and Dad, even while they shook Underskinker's hand.

"In fact, Coach," said the first suit, "we have something for you."

He bent over and reached into his briefcase. He took out an ugly, cheap-looking gold plastic statuette. There was a little tag on the bottom, which he flicked off with his pocketknife. The tag went skittering across the floor, and Justin picked it up.

"Here you go, Coach. In recognition," the first suit said, handing it to Underskinker.

"We better be going," the second suit said. "Good to meet you, Coach. Principal Horvath, don't worry about a thing."

"Please allow me to escort you gentlemen off our campus," Horvath said.

Off they went, between Horvath and Charon.

Underskinker looked down at the statuette.

"Dis is duh most beautiful ting I ever saw in my life," he said. "You punks . . . you punks . . ." He turned away and went back to his office.

"Dad," I said. "How?"

"Son, the fact that I am a lawyer does not make me a complete idiot. Remember, I went to law school in this state. And one of my classmates was a jenti girl from New Sodom. She didn't tell me much, and I didn't believe what I heard, but it became obvious even to me that there was more going on here than anybody was willing to speak about openly. I mean, how many towns have a resident population of giants in sunglasses? Well, I was willing to do what New England does best and say nothing. Things were going pretty well, I thought. As long as I was making money hand over fist and you were here at Vlad, I was satisfied. But that day when we went to the movie theater and were treated like visiting royalty—and it was clear to me it was because of you—I knew something was going on. Something that I had to know more about. Antonescu told me a little. I learned a little more on my own. But it's only today that I've begun to realize how much reason I have to be proud of you."

And he hugged me, even though I was still wet.

After a minute, I thought of something.

"Dad," I said, "quarter grades are out in a week. I don't think mine are going to be very good."

Dad just went on hugging me.

After he left, I hung around a little while longer, hoping for one particular person to come up to me, but she was nowhere in sight. Finally, when I decided she wasn't coming and would never come, I went back into the locker room to change.

Justin followed me back. He was his old self now, dry and shy. But he had a wicked grin on his face.

"Look what was on that trophy they gave Coach Underskinker," he said, and held the tag out to me:

To Coach Aloysius Ryan
and the St. Biddulph's Saints
Water Polo Team
From the State of Massachusetts
with Gratitude

"You sure messed things up for the state," Justin said. "They were all set to start closing us down."

"I guess." I shrugged. Now that it was over, it didn't seem to matter as much. I was still glad that they weren't going to close Vlad Dracul, but now I didn't have anything to think about but Ileana.

We heard a deep snore.

"We should check on Underskinker," I said.

We went back to the office and saw our coach with his feet up on his desk and a peaceful look on his face. The trophy was tucked under his arm like a baby doll.

THE QUEEN OF ILLYRIA

The next day at free period, the natatorium was crowded with jenti. All the little, quiet, brown-haired or blond ones who went through the halls without being noticed were lining up to see if they could turn into selkies when they got in the water. The school had a doctor and two nurses waiting by the pool as the jenti kids eased into the shallow end and slowly put their faces down, while Justin and I stood by on either side of them.

Every one of them changed. Every one of them was a natural swimmer. From now on, Vlad Dracul wouldn't need to find gadje to fake its water sports programs. Their teams would be the best in the state.

Of course, that meant everybody would have to admit that vampires were not something out of folklore or that

216

Bram Stoker made up. They were just a different kind of people.

After that, it seemed like everything at Vlad Dracul started to change. The jenti began smiling at each other, even waving. And they didn't always wear their sunglasses. They didn't really need them much more than anybody else.

People started coming to me for advice about how to "misbehave in true gadje fashion." That was interesting.

When I described spit wads, two kids in a physics class actually made some. Then they developed a launcher, recorded the flight characteristics, and turned it all in for extra credit.

When I told them in social studies about cutting class, everyone suddenly stood up and marched six blocks away to an ice cream store, where one of them announced, "Hello. We are not supposed to be here. May we have vanilla cones to go, please?"

They didn't really get the point of it, though. They brought Mr. Gibbon along.

Gregor was even sent to Horvath's office for playing a boom box in the student union with the volume turned all the way up. (He'd been playing a Bach cantata, but hey.)

"I was experimenting," he told Horvath. "I had been given to understand it was a youthful gadje behavior."

All Horvath did was ask him not to do it again.

One day, the whole varsity football team turned themselves into wolves and went to class like that. Then they insisted that the name of their team be changed to the Werewolves, and Horvath let them do it. He had new jackets for them the next day.

Because Horvath was changing, too.

He announced that starting next year, Vlad Dracul would be open to academically gifted students from all over the United States, even gadje. If there was enough demand, the school would build a new dorm to handle the overflow.

It was also announced that a nationwide search for a new water-sports coach would be made over the summer. Coach Underskinker would be promoted at the end of the year to a position Horvath was creating, Supervisor of Locker Access. There would be a big pay increase.

Pyrek, Falbo, and Tracy were informed that they had met the requirements for graduation a year or two early and would get their diplomas with that year's senior class. They were offered full athletic scholarships to a huge Baptist college in Texas. I don't know if they went there or not.

And downtown started to change. Not in any dramatic way—unless you knew the history of New Sodom—but at least people started going into each other's stores. I knew things were different the first time I saw a sign in the window of the local jeans outlet: WE NOW STOCK EXTRA EXTRA TALL. Right across from it, Aurari's bookstore was putting in a clear glass window.

All of this was very interesting in a way, but it didn't cheer me up as much as it might have. Because as far as I could tell, Princess Ileana didn't notice.

Then came the last Friday in May.

It was a beautiful day. Everything was blooming, and there was heat in the air. Summer was close enough to touch.

I went to the library and waited for Justin to get done

with his shelving. For no particular reason, I picked up a copy of *Dracula* and flipped through it. I'd read the book during the winter, and I'd been wondering ever since why Stoker had put everything down so wrong. Jenti had made friends with him, shared things with him. Maybe they'd hoped he'd write a book that would introduce them to the world as they really were, as a first step toward coming out of their shadows. Maybe. But he'd taken every one of the things that made them powerful and special and turned them into evil. Why? What sense did it make?

I wondered if he'd just been jealous.

When Justin was finished, he came over and got me.

"Good-bye, boys!" Ms. Shadwell howled after us. For a librarian, she sure was noisy.

"Come on," Justin said. "I want to go down by the creek."

So we walked across campus in the late-afternoon sun and somehow, for the first time since I'd come to Massachusetts, I felt I belonged someplace. I wouldn't go so far as to say that I liked it. But so much had happened since that cold January day when Dad and I had driven up that I was part of this school now, like it or not. Of course, it probably helped that the year was almost over and I wouldn't be coming back for three months.

The trees that grew along the creek made it a river of shade now. Anyway, it was a river to a Californian. The green darkness was beautiful, and the light that found its way down the banks was as soft as—well, as soft as Ileana's lips on my cheek.

"That's better," Justin said, taking off the dark glasses he still wore on bright days, like most jenti.

We walked down the creek, me with my eyes on the trees, Justin looking where we were stepping, until we came to a big rock. This rock was so big that the creek had to bend to go around it. It was flat on top, and the shadows of the trees made patterns on its sides.

Up on top of it was Ileana.

"Hello," she said.

"Hey," I said, trying to sound cool. "How come you don't have a piano lesson?"

"Mrs. Warrener moved my lesson to tomorrow," Ileana said. "What are you doing down here?"

"I don't know." Justin shrugged. "We just felt like coming."

"Perhaps you would like to climb up here with me," Ileana said.

We climbed up the rock and all sat in a row, watching the creek. It was different now than it had been in January, when Gregor and his gang had tried to dump Justin into it. It was wide and fast and sounded happy. The sun glinted off its back like it was smiling.

Justin crawled to the edge of the rock and looked down at it.

"Wonder what it would be like to swim in that," he said.

"You can't. It's too shallow," I said.

"Gets deeper farther down," Justin said. "See you. Won't be long."

And he scampered down the rock and out of sight in a flash.

Which left me alone with Ileana. And her alone with me.

We just sat side by side without looking at each other for a while.

Finally she said, "I asked Justin to bring you here."

"Oh," I said.

"I wanted to tell you that I apologize. I should not have been so angry with you over Gregor. I should have known that you were only defending Justin. You would never hide behind the mark I put on you. It was wrong of me to think that you ever would do something so ignoble."

"No, you were right, I was out of line," I said. "But I have apologized to Gregor."

"I heard," she said. "Of course you would." She sighed and went on.

"You have done so much, Cody. You helped Justin over and over again, and by doing so you have now helped all jenti to feel less afraid. Water is a great terror to us. If even a few of us can live in it, it makes us think anything might be possible. I think you must be the greatest gadje friend the jenti have ever had.

"I am not worthy to ask this," she went on. "But . . . is it possible that we might be friends again?"

And right then, on that rock, with the creek going by, and the frogs singing, and the shadows making the light come and go on the most beautiful face in the world, I had the best moment of my life so far. It was so perfect, I didn't even want to speak. I didn't want to move. I didn't want it to end.

But I had to do something to let her know. So I kissed her. And this time I didn't miss.

"There's one thing you'd better know," I said. "That stuff I read you from my poem that you thought was so funny? It wasn't supposed to be. That's the best I can do. I'm just not a poet."

Ileana shook her head. "That book you gave me for my birthday was a poem," she said. "A very fine one. And so was going to Justin and giving him your blood. Vasco would have done so for Anaxander."

And she kissed me back.

We just stayed there, the two of us, until the sun left us and the rock got cold. Then Justin came back, and we went up through the trees back onto the main part of the campus.

Ileana and I were still holding hands.

The lights were on in the dorms and the student union, but the other buildings were dark. Their high, flat roofs stood out against the spring light that still clung to the sky high up.

Charon came toward us out of the shadows, his eyes gleaming. His tail made a kind of swish I hadn't seen before.

But Ileana must have, because she said, "Yes, we are fine, Charon. We were down by the creek. Now we are going home. Good night."

Charon moved off a little but kept pace with us.

"Is he mad?" I asked.

"Not at all," Ileana said. "It's just that Charon's real work starts at darkness, when he patrols the campus all night long. He wants to see us safely off it. He is very responsible. Wolves are often like that."

Justin was walking a little way ahead of us. On purpose, I was willing to bet. Good old Justin. He could play a trick like this on me anytime.

"Right now, this has got to be the most beautiful place in the world," I said in a low voice.

"More beautiful than California?" Ileana asked.

"More beautiful than anywhere."

We stood there and held each other for what must have been a long time.

Charon sat down a little way off. I felt like he was guarding our privacy.

"You must know, Cody, that not all of the jenti are happy with what is happening," Ileana said. "The younger people, yes, but the older ones are frightened. They do not know where it will end."

"You mean, like your parents?" I asked.

"Yes," Ileana said.

"I think there will be no trouble," said a deep voice beside us.

I looked over at Charon. All I could see now was his eyes. And they were slowly rising in the air. In a moment, they were looking down on us from nearly eight feet up. I could hear a leathery rustle that sounded like wings.

Ileana gasped. "What are you doing here?"

"Keeping an eye on my favorite descendant's only child," the eyes said.

Ileana curtsied.

"My mother did not tell me you were watching over me," she said.

"Only Horvath knew," the eyes replied. "That was my intention."

"I wish I had known," Ileana said. "I feel that you think I am untrustworthy."

"Don't be foolish, child," said the voice. "Being a

princess of the jenti is burden enough. If you had known that the founder of your family was living on the campus, that would have been one more reason for you always to be on guard against yourself. I did not want that."

"So, obviously, you're not a Canadian timber wolf," I interrupted.

"No," the voice said. "That was the story I gave to Horvath to tell others. My real name is known to you. I am Dracula."

I didn't say anything. I just looked up at those deep yellow eyes. Then one of them winked.

"Cody Elliot. I have been watching you since you came among us. In your rather silly way, you have shown much courage and generosity. I admire such things. Not since Bram Stoker have I trusted a gadje. But I trust you. I trust you with that which is most precious to me, my many-greats-granddaughter, who is the night rose of her people. The old ways have preserved us in a world that has feared and hated us for centuries. And not without reason. But this is a different country. Things are changing and have changed. And you, my dear boy, have done more to change them in five months than they have changed since I was a very young man indeed.

"Descendant, I am well pleased with this gadje boy," Dracula went on. "You are both young, and much may happen. You may grow together or you may part and go on to even truer loves. I do not know. But you may keep him if you wish."

"Respectfully, ancestor, if you told me I could not, I would do so anyway," Ileana said. "And I would not permit you to prevent it."

Dracula laughed, and the ground shook.

"The answer I was hoping for! You have my blood in rich measure."

Out of the dark, a huge, heavy hand found mine and clasped it.

I felt a thick claw gently scraping a design on my cheek.

"This will save much talk and trouble with Ileana's parents. As for your parents, I'm afraid you are on your own."

"Don't worry," I said.

"I do not," Dracula said. "And now, descendant, good-bye for a while. Now that you know who Charon is, there is no reason for me to keep to that form. And school is nearly out, anyway. I will spend the summer in Carpathia with old friends. In the fall, I will return to see how everything is getting on. Say hello to your parents for me."

There was a breath of air as he spread his wings, and I could hear them growing as he changed shape again.

"Seventeen meters," he announced. "The old bat can still spread."

There was a heavy downbeat of wind, then another, and against the risen moon, I saw one flash of wings.

Finally Ileana said, "We had better catch up to Justin."

LAST CHAPTER

And that was pretty much everything that happened up to this point. It was Ileana who gave me the idea to write it all down and hand it in for a grade in English. She and Justin both helped me with it, remembering everything and typing it up. They helped me a lot with the style, too. But the writing is mine.

It's not an epic, and it's not three hundred pages, not even close, but, Mr. Shadwell, I know you'll grade it as if it was a jenti's work.

Cody Elliot

Roman à clef? Bildungsroman? I'm not quite certain how to categorize this text, but I take pleasure in assigning it a well-earned jenti C.

N. P. Shadwell